CRUISE INTO DARKNESS

A RACHEL PRINCE MYSTERY
BOOK 14

DAWN BROOKES

CRUISE INTO DARKNESS

This novel is entirely a work of fiction. The names, characters and incidents portrayed are the work of the author's imagination, except for those in the public domain. Any resemblance to actual persons, living or dead, is entirely coincidental. Although real-life places are depicted in settings, all situations and people related to those places are fictional.

DAWN BROOKES asserts the moral right to be identified as the author of this work. All rights reserved in all media. No part of this publication may be reproduced, stored in a retrieval system, or transmitted, in any form, or by any means, electronic, mechanical, photocopying, recording or otherwise, without the prior written permission of the author and/or publisher.

Paperback Edition 2025
Kindle Edition 2025
Paperback ISBN: 978-1-916842-18-2
Hardback ISBN: 978-1-916842-19-9
Copyright © DAWN BROOKES 2025
Cover Images: Adobe Stock Images
Cover Design: John & Janet

The light shines in the darkness, and the darkness has not overcome it.
(John 1:5)

1

The ship lurched violently, sending a water bottle crashing to the floor of Rachel Jacobi-Prince's stateroom. In her dream, she had been running through a landscape of jagged mountains, trying to escape a killer. The sharp pain erupting in her temple was no longer a part of the nightmare, but rather a brutal reality yanking her back to consciousness.

Rachel's eyes shot open. Darkness enveloped her. Her hand instinctively reached for her phone as she shook her head to clear the disorientation between sleep and wakefulness. The phone wasn't there. Instead, her fingers brushed against the carpet on the tilting floor. She had been thrown out of bed.

Another violent pitch sent her sliding. Her shoulder slammed into something solid. With pain coursing through her shoulder and upper arm, Rachel realised what was happening. The storm the *Coral Queen* had been trying to outrun had caught up with them. Feeling the ship reeling, she braced herself this time, clinging to a fixed desk leg to defy gravity. As the ship was battered by the storm, she could feel the engines running at full throttle, desperately trying to escape. Shouts of alarm, thuds of falling furniture, and occasional yelps of fear and pain echoed from the corridor. The evening before, most passengers had been offered free doses of anti-sickness medication, and Rachel was grateful she had followed medical advice and got an injection. To be fair, it had been more of an order from Captain Peter Jenson and Dr Graham Bentley, neither of whom wanted senior officers incapacitated by motion sickness if the storm did hit.

And hit it had.

Rachel gritted her teeth as she manoeuvred onto her knees and crawled toward the curtains, which were closer than any light switches. She pulled the drapes open and immediately wished she hadn't; the view was nothing short of apocalyptic. Massive waves hurled themselves against the windows of deck six, transforming her view into a stomach-churning mess until the ship rolled to the other side. How on earth would it get through this? A bolt of lightning split the sky, followed almost immediately by an enormous boom of thunder that made her heart pound. She had never been a fan of thunderstorms, except from a distance. This one was far too close!

Rachel struggled to her feet and took a few tentative steps toward a light switch. When the lights flickered on, her hand went to her temple, where she felt the sticky trickle of blood.

"Great. Just great." She rotated her shoulder; it felt sore, but the movement assured her it wasn't broken.

Another sudden clap of thunder crashed around her. The sound, louder than anything she had ever heard, seemed to shake the very bones of the luxurious cruise liner. Taking advantage of the next roll, Rachel allowed herself to be thrown toward the bathroom but this time she used the momentum to control her direction. Pulling the bathroom door open, she clambered inside, checking her head in the mirror while gripping the sink to steady herself. The source of the blood was a deep cut above her right temple. Under normal circumstances, she would head straight to the medical centre, but something told her they would be overwhelmed. Not to mention how difficult it would be to get there while the storm continued to rage.

DIY treatment it is, then, she thought, a grim smile crossing her face. Rachel grabbed a hand towel and pressed it to her head as the ship continued its violent dance on the ocean. She was getting used to it, moving with its rhythm while rifling through a medicine bag with her free hand. She found what she was looking for, washed and dried the wound as best she could, pinched it together with her fingers and then added medicinal glue to the top. Satisfied the treatment would contain the bleeding, she tossed some towels into the bath and climbed inside. At least it was safe, she reasoned. Finding a suitable dressing in her medical bag, she applied it to her head using a hand mirror. She grinned. Not pretty, but it will do. You'll be proud of me when I see you, Sarah. Or maybe not.

Thinking of her best friend, who was a nurse on the medical team, and how chaotic it would be around the ship, Rachel examined her damaged arm and shoulder. "Ouch, you're going to have a nasty bruise there." Debating whether to apply arnica, something her mother swore prevented bruising, Rachel accepted she would be unlikely to find any, and decided it was more important to get dressed and help around the ship.

The ship continued to be bounced around like a beach ball while Rachel waited for a temporary lull. By lull, she meant a less acute list. When one came, she climbed out of the bath, hurried into the stateroom, and found the crisp white uniform that was always waiting in case she was called to an emergency in the middle of the night. There had been plenty of those since she joined the ship as chief of security, but thankfully, nothing too serious to date.

Once dressed in her pristine whites, she fastened her long blonde hair into a ponytail. Apart from the dressing on her head, which her cap almost covered, she looked ready for anything. Her phone wasn't where she'd left it when she went to sleep. The plug lay on the floor, wrenched from its socket, but the phone wasn't attached. It must have been thrown under the bed. Rachel got to the floor just in time because another gigantic crash hit her side of the ship, and she would have lost her footing anyway. After that and another terrifying thunderclap passed, Rachel found what she was looking for and put it in her pocket. She attached her radio to her waistband and made for the door but was thrown back onto the bed. The ship reeled and listed for another ten minutes as the storm appeared to be right overhead. She felt the ship's emergency systems stop the engines, as they did in severe weather. They were now at the mercy of the sea. A sudden silence was followed by an enormous crack of lightning before everything went black.

Rachel waited for the ship's generator and secondary systems to kick in, but they didn't. The thunder and lightning passed, and the ship was mostly silent in the eerie darkness. Apart from the creaking and groaning as the remaining storm waves tossed it about, it remained that way for what felt like an eternity. The silence was even more terrifying than the storm. She pulled her phone from her pocket, but the screen was dark. How could that be? Was it some sort of electromagnetic interference? Not knowing what time it was and unable to get her phone working, Rachel fumbled in the dark, reaching into a drawer for a torch. She had been told the systems were failsafe and that what was happening could never occur. So much for that theory.

Using the torch to guide herself to the balcony doors, she found everything outside was pitch black. The stars weren't visible because of the clouds. It was the stuff of nightmares. Something felt very off. A shudder ran down her spine as Rachel reached for her radio. Surely that would work. Nope. "This is ridiculous," she muttered, thinking of the engineering guy who had assured her the ship's technological failsafes would never let this sort of thing happen. "Just wait until I see him."

Rachel moved unsteadily toward her door. The corridor outside was a mass of darkness. Not even the emergency lights that were supposed to guide people to lifeboats in case of a call to muster stations were lit.

Taking a deep breath, Rachel realised the engines had cut out, and the ship was sailing blind.

2

Almost as suddenly as the power had cut, it came on again. "Better late than never," she murmured. There were surprisingly few people wandering the corridors, considering what had just happened. She imagined most of them were in hiding, waiting for the nightmare to end. She smiled reassuringly at those she passed as the engines started up again and those on the bridge took control. "Looks like we've moved out of the storm's path. You can go back to bed now."

Rachel half expected Peter Jenson to make an announcement, but now she could see her phone, it was three o'clock in the morning. He had warned the passengers many hours ago that they might not be able to outrun the storm and that if it hit, they were to stay put unless they heard otherwise.

Rachel's radio crackled to life. Both it and Jason Goodridge's voice were welcome. "Hi Jason, how's—"

"Rachel. I'm in main laundry. You'd better get down here." The urgency in his voice was clear enough for her not to ask questions.

"On my way," she said.

The ship continued to sway when Rachel entered the laundry area, though not as violently as it had done fifteen minutes earlier.

Dr Graham Bentley and her best friend, Sarah Bradshaw, were on the scene. It was clear to Rachel that there was nothing to be done for the person they were assessing. The woman, who appeared to be in her early thirties, lay sprawled across the conveyor belt used for pressing clean sheets. She wore an officer's white uniform with three gold stripes on the epaulettes, indicating she was a senior officer of the same rank as Rachel, but she didn't recognise her. Her light brown hair was pinned back, though slightly dishevelled, and her blue eyes were wide open. The life they had once embodied was no longer present. A small gold cross hung around her neck.

"Who is she, Graham?" Rachel asked.

"We don't know," said Graham. Rachel still found it odd calling the senior medical officer by his first name, but now that she was of equal rank, it was expected.

"She's not crew, although at first glance you would

have thought so," said Sarah. "The uniform's a reasonable match, but there are differences."

Rachel raised an eyebrow. "Looks the same to me."

"The labels don't belong to the company we use, and the jacket doesn't have the same number of buttons. Unfortunately, she's not carrying any ID to tell us who she really is," said Graham.

"Do you think she's a passenger in fancy dress?" Rachel asked.

Graham moved away from the body. "Not likely. All events were cancelled last night, and passengers were warned to stay away from public areas in case the storm caught up with us. You could check with Nat..." Natalie Rodriguez had been promoted to cruise director after her predecessor was sacked for inappropriate behaviour. "...and ask if any fancy dress parties were planned. We have to assume she's a passenger, but I don't know why or how she ended up here. Initial appearances suggest she got knocked over during the storm."

Rachel made a note on her phone to look into the fancy dress element.

Sarah caught Rachel's eye. "How did you cope with your first horror storm?"

Rachel pulled her cap off, revealing the dressing. "Not without drama, but I glued myself together."

"I wondered why you were wearing your cap. We should take a look at that," said Sarah, heading her way.

"Later," said Rachel. "How did our Jane Doe die?"

"Her neck's broken," said Graham, shaking his head. "I expect you'll want to check for yourselves and take photos. Do you mind if we leave you to it? I promise I'll examine her thoroughly in the morgue. We've taken blood samples and swabs, but there's no more we can do here, and there are lots of passengers to attend to."

"Of course. We'll arrange for the body to be moved to the morgue once we're finished here," said Rachel. "Is that the person who found her?" Rachel noticed an older man sitting in a chair, trembling. Ravanos, a member of the security team, was interviewing him and taking notes.

Jason Goodridge, Rachel's deputy and Sarah's husband, ushered Rachel to one side. "He thinks our mystery woman fell, and we're letting him believe that for now."

Rachel exhaled. "Are you saying she didn't fall?"

Jason shook his head. "This was a professional job, made to look like an accident. I saw a lot of bruises like those on the back of her neck, on the battlefield. She was murdered, Rachel."

"Show me."

Jason gently turned the woman onto her side, revealing telltale thumb marks. There were no other bruises or cuts indicative of a fall. "Okay." She walked over to the crewman, raising a quizzical eyebrow at Ravanos.

Ravanos spoke to the man in what sounded like Spanish and then, in English, to Rachel. "He came to check on the machinery once the lights came on and found her like this. He doesn't speak English, Chief."

"Is he Italian?"

"No, he's from El Salvador and speaks Spanish; I know enough of the language to understand his account. He's confirmed the dead woman doesn't work here."

"Did he see anybody else when he arrived?"

"No. But he thought he heard a clang when he entered. It could have been the equipment firing up after the power outage."

"Where did this clang come from?"

Ravanos didn't need to translate; the man obviously understood English even though he didn't speak it.

"He can't be sure. It echoes down here."

"Okay. Let him go for now. Tell him I'm sorry he's had such a shock and to get a strong coffee. We may need to speak to him again. This area's out of bounds for a while."

The man started jabbering at Ravanos in Spanish.

"He says they have work to do and the pressing machine is vital."

"I understand, but we'll need at least an hour. We'll be as quick as we can." Rachel didn't want the man adding to the stress of the hospitality chief any more than the storm would have done. There would be a lot of frayed tempers and injured crew for her to deal with as it was.

The man left them to it, muttering and murmuring now that he had recovered from the initial shock of finding a dead person. Rachel returned to where the woman was lying. Jason was already taking photos from every angle. "Shall I put up a cordon, Chief?" Ravanos asked.

"No. Just stop anyone coming in and look around. See if you can find anything that might make a clanging sound."

Rachel donned gloves and looked at the well-dressed young woman with porcelain skin. She was wearing a smartwatch. "That might tell us something, Jason."

Jason bagged the watch while Rachel surveyed the woman. "Who are you and what were you doing down here?" Rachel asked.

"She could have got lost," said Jason, snapping a few more pictures while Rachel moved the woman from side to side.

"Then why the uniform? The doors are all labelled with crew-only signs."

"An assignation, maybe?" Jason quizzed.

"Possible. But the uniform and the absence of ID suggest she was pretending to be someone she wasn't. If she was meeting someone, we need to find out who. Did something get out of hand?"

Chapter 2

"Or maybe I'm being paranoid, and it was an accident. It could have happened when the power went off."

Rachel remembered the judder as the ship had come to a sudden stop before the blackout. "So why leave her?"

"Whoever she was meeting could have been scared they would lose their job."

"Or be arrested for murder," said Rachel. "Both plausible. Let's keep an open mind for now and keep our suspicions quiet. Our priority is to find out who she was."

Ravanos returned from his search of the corridors. "There's nothing out of the ordinary."

"What about the clanging sound?"

"What clanging?" Jason raised an eyebrow.

"The crewman thought he heard a clanging sound when he came in," said Rachel.

Jason turned on his heel. "Follow me."

Rachel and Ravanos followed Jason around a corner and watched in astonishment as he lifted a grooved metal hatch, almost invisible as it blended in with the metal floor. He climbed inside, dropping the hatch after him. A loud clang filled their ears. Jason pushed the hatch open again from underneath the floor, grinning widely.

"An old hand showed me this not long after I started. Few people know about it now because, in the past, it was used for all sorts of activities from skiving to—"

"I get the picture," said Rachel. "Does it lead anywhere?"

"For those in the know, it's a shortcut to the M1, and from there…" he shrugged. The M1 was so named by Brits because it ran the length of the ship. Americans called it the I95 for the same reason.

"From there, the person could have gone anywhere. If foul play is involved, it's likely somebody who knew about this hatch and how to get around the ship. It has to be crew."

"That's a reasonable assumption," said Jason. "Although, if this woman had a meeting with a member of our crew and wound up dead, I don't like the idea at all."

"Ravanos, take one last look around and pick up anything that might offer us clues as to whom the woman met or ran into. Also, arrange for the body to be moved to the morgue. Make sure whoever collects her wears forensic overalls, gloves, and boots. Dr Bentley will conduct a more thorough examination when he has more time. Once she's gone and you're satisfied we've checked everything, get someone to wash down the conveyor belt and let the crew inside. Jason and I are going for a wander through the secret tunnel." She lowered herself into the tunnel and closed the hatch. "How come I didn't know about this?"

"Sorry, Rachel. I should have told you."

"No. The person who gave me the full ship tour should have told me."

"Unless they didn't know about it. Although I bet everyone who works in the laundry knows it's here, along with most of the senior officers. Secrets are hard to keep on board the *Coral Queen*."

Rachel rubbed her temple, then winced. "Ouch. I forgot that was there. I'm going to have to develop a new thinking habit."

Using Rachel's torch and Jason's phone torch, they searched for clues as they walked. Rachel soon realised that inside this tunnel, it was an entirely different world. Narrow pipes ran along the ceiling and walls, some sweating condensation that dripped intermittently onto the metal grate beneath their feet. The air was thick with a complex bouquet of scents: stale machine oil, hot metal, a hint of industrial-strength cleaning solution, and something else Rachel couldn't quite place. Beneath her feet, the metal vibrated with the ship's distant heartbeat, a constant low-frequency hum that seemed to resonate through her bones. Bare lightbulbs hung at irregular intervals, casting pools of dim, yellowish light that created more shadows than they dispelled. Electrical conduits and hydraulic lines snaked across the walls, forming a labyrinthine network that spoke of the complex inner workings of the massive vessel. The occasional distant clang or mechanical whir echoed through the tunnel, a reminder that they were moving through a part of the ship's hidden circulatory system – its veins, except this was supposed to be a secret passage.

Jason chuckled as she followed him along a narrow and dimly lit tunnel. The ship had myriads of access tunnels and maintenance areas where someone in the know could hide, but this was different. "Was it designed as a shortcut or for maintenance?" she asked.

"I'm not sure of its original purpose, but it's out of bounds now. Unless, of course, something breaks down here."

"A great escape route for someone intent on committing murder, though."

"Which would make it premeditated, but it could also have been used by someone who panicked when they found her," said Jason.

"Of course, it might not have been used at all, and the clanging could have come from something else when the ship's power returned, like the crewman thought. I'll tell you what, though, it feels a lot calmer down here than it does upstairs. Maybe we should hide until the storm has completely passed," Rachel said with a grin.

"Yeah. As if that would work for an adrenaline junkie."

"You know me too well." Rachel enjoyed working with Jason. She had known him for a long time as a

Chapter 2

friend, but working with him as her deputy had allowed her to experience a different side of him. He was the perfect number two, although she still didn't understand why he hadn't taken the job as senior when her predecessor, Jack Waverley, had offered it to him. She missed seeing Waverley around now that she was working on board the *Coral Queen*. She hadn't asked Jason what he had been like to work with, because Jason was loyal to a fault, and she wouldn't want to put him in that position. When the time was right, she would ask Rosemary Inglis, someone she had got to know during previous investigations when Rachel had been a civilian passenger, albeit while working as a detective in the UK. Only six weeks before, she had taken a long overdue furlough from that job, and she and her husband, Carlos, had toured Scotland for three weeks before she boarded the cruise ship as their new chief of security. Sometimes she had to pinch herself, as it all seemed a lifetime away. If she was honest, she was loving her new role and life aboard the ship, except for missing Carlos.

"What's this?"

Jason came to a stop just ahead of her. "What?"

Rachel bent down and picked up a micro-SD card from the floor that, luckily, hadn't fallen through the grate; otherwise, she'd never have spotted it. She held it up. "It could belong to anyone, but you never know, we might get lucky. It's worth inspecting." She dropped it into a different evidence bag from the smartwatch. Having worked in the police force, she was all too aware of how easy it was to contaminate evidence.

"Well spotted," said Jason. "We're almost there now. Do you want me to come back with a more powerful torch and search properly?"

"As it's the only lead we've got so far, yes, please. Although our killer could have exited by a normal entrance."

"Not if they were disturbed by the laundry guy. This remains the most logical escape route." Jason pushed open a door, and they entered the familiar M1. Once he closed the door, she saw how well hidden the tunnel was from this side. Jason showed her a tiny latch accessible with one finger.

The M1 corridor was well lit, and a few of the night shift workers had started moving supplies. She guessed they were behind due to the storm, which had made it too dangerous before now.

3

The ship listed starboard, sending Sarah stumbling against a fixed table. "Ouch!" she cried, as pain shot through her thigh. Her right leg had crashed into the edge, the contact just above her knee.

Sarah was taking a shortcut through the main restaurant to the M1 corridor via the rear entrance. The usually elegant Coral Restaurant was empty of passengers and waiting staff. Chairs were strapped together and secured around the edges of the room, their rich burgundy upholstery still visible under the dim lighting. All non-fixed tables had been moved and tied down to prevent them from becoming projectiles during the storm. Her medical bag swung wildly from her left shoulder like a pendulum.

The storm was easing, but Sarah's aching feet and the constant pitching and rolling told her it wasn't yet over. Every so often, a rogue wave slammed against the ship's hull, the impact reverberating through the structure like a giant's fist. She'd lost count of the number of passengers she'd treated for seasickness or injuries in the hours since the woman's body had been found in the laundry – a discovery she was trying hard not to think about. Most of the injuries she'd treated had been minor sprains, cuts, and bruises from people losing their balance or being caught off guard by the ship's erratic movements. Her radio crackled constantly with calls to visit another passenger or crew member too afraid to venture to the medical centre. The medical team was stretched thin, with the senior nurse, Gwen Sumner, holding the fort in the infirmary while two nurses and Janet, the junior doctor, held emergency surgeries and the rest of the team treated passengers throughout the ship's sixteen decks.

Thunder cracked overhead like a celestial whip, making her jump despite her years at sea. The crystal chandeliers swayed, and the bulbs flickered ominously. This wasn't her first storm, or even her worst – that dubious honour belonged to a category four hurricane off the coast of Florida two years earlier, but it was the first time the ship's failsafe systems hadn't kicked in following a power cut. Three bursts of the ship's horn made her jump, the deep, resonant sound cutting through the background noise of wind and waves.

Planting her feet apart on the carpeted floor, Sarah

regained her balance. The wide stance she had learned became second nature during rough weather. All crew were taught how to stay on their feet during a storm, and mostly, the training worked. Sarah's thigh throbbed where she'd hit it, and she made a mental note to grab an extra ice pack when she had a moment – whenever that might be. She teetered through the restaurant again, one hand trailing along the fixed tables for support, the other trying to control her bag.

A muffled groan near the exit to the M1 grabbed Sarah's attention. Close to the crew-only area, a man in his late twenties was slumped against the wall, one hand braced against the polished surface of a rail while the other clutched his right shoulder. Sarah pushed aside her exhaustion.

"Sir? Are you hurt?" she called out, already moving toward him on instinct.

The man looked up, startled. Rain or sea spray had soaked through his white shirt, plastering it to his skin in a way that reminded Sarah of the tissue-paper-thin hospital gowns she'd worked with during her NHS days. A lifetime ago. A tear in his shirt sleeve revealed an angry red scrape that looked painful but superficial.

"I'm fine," he said, though his grimace betrayed his actual condition. "Just lost my balance for a minute." His appearance was mixed Hispanic, but his accent was distinctly British, casual and educated, the kind of voice she associated with a BBC documentary.

Sarah noted how he held his shoulder and the careful way he was controlling his breathing – classic signs of someone trying to manage significant pain. "That looks like it might be dislocated. I'm Sarah Bradshaw, one of the ship's nurses. Let me look."

He hesitated, brown eyes darting toward the restricted area. A flash of lightning illuminated his face, highlighting a small scar above his right eyebrow, old and long since healed.

"Really, it's unnecessary—" Another violent wave sent him stumbling, and he couldn't suppress a gasp of pain that cut through his protests.

"Nevertheless, I'd like to be sure," she said firmly, setting down her medical bag. "What's your name?"

"Alex. Alex Reyes." He offered a smile that seemed as practiced as hers and professional, but it didn't quite remove the tension in his shoulders. Sarah had worked with enough patients to recognise when someone was trying too hard to appear casual.

"Well, Alex, you seem to be going the wrong way. That's crew-only through there, so you wouldn't have got much further. What brought you down here at this hour?"

His fingers twitched against his thigh – he appeared nervous, which was at odds with his composed though pained, expression. "I got disorientated trying to get lower down. I'm on the fourteenth floor..."

He hesitated, and Sarah filled the pause while

opening her medical bag. "It can be rougher on the higher decks." She should know; she'd spent most of her time on the higher decks as the storm did its worst.

"Yeah, when it hit, I panicked..." He shrugged, then winced, the movement clearly causing him pain.

Sarah pulled out her pen torch. "Follow the light with your eyes, please." He complied without argument, and she found no signs of concussion. His soft brown eyes appeared anxious but tracked the light as they should. "We should get you to the medical centre—"

"No!" The word shot out sharply, but then Alex modulated his tone. "I mean, couldn't you just check it here? I don't want to make a fuss."

The ship creaked ominously around them, the sound of straining metal loud in the relative quiet of the abandoned restaurant. Sarah noticed his hands were smooth, but for subtle calluses on his fingertips, the kind that came from hours at a keyboard. Not the hands of someone who did manual labour.

"This isn't the place." Another thunderclap rattled through the restaurant. Alex flinched, but Sarah noticed his eyes weren't focused on the ceiling; they were fixed on something past her shoulder, toward the crew area he definitely shouldn't have been near.

"Please," he mumbled. "I'd rather not have this documented."

"I'm sorry, but all passenger injuries have to be reported." His reactions were sending warning signals through her mind, like the beeping of a patient monitor before things went wrong. But there was something in Alex's expression; not a threat, rather genuine distress that made her hesitate. "At least let me check if the shoulder's dislocated," she said.

He nodded, and Sarah noticed how his breathing became more controlled.

Sarah reached for his shoulder, moving her good knee onto the carpet.

He sat back against the wall, remaining unusually still as she examined him, too still for someone who claimed to have been panicked by the storm. The shoulder wasn't dislocated, but the muscles were strained and beginning to swell. The scrape on his arm revealed an unusual pattern, almost geometric in its precision. He saw her looking and covered it up. "It's nothing," he said.

"You'll need ice and compression," Sarah said, pulling cold gel supplies from her bag. "And I really should cover—"

A distant crash echoed from the other side of the restaurant, followed by the sound of running feet. It caught their attention. Alex's muscles tensed beneath her hands, his eyes widening fractionally before he controlled his expression once more. Sarah recognised the subtle shift in his muscles. He was frightened.

"Thank you for your help," he said quickly, pulling

away, despite her unfinished treatment. "I appreciate your help, but I should get back to my cabin."

"Wait." But he was already moving, his gait smooth despite the ship's motion, suggesting he was more comfortable at sea than the average passenger. Maybe he cruised a lot. Sarah watched him disappear out of the restaurant, questions confusing her. Was Alex Reyes simply a passenger who'd got lost during a storm, or was there something more to his presence near the crew area, on this night of all nights?

"Nurse Sarah." The voice broke through her thoughts. Maria, one of the servers she recognised, hurried towards her, her eyes wild. "Come quickly. A passenger... she collapsed."

Sarah gathered her medical bag, pushing the thoughts of Alex Reyes aside as she followed the anxious woman to the other side of the restaurant. An elderly woman lay on the floor, her silver hair fanned out against the dark red carpet.

"Madam?" The woman groaned as Sarah knelt beside her new patient, reaching for her stethoscope. She feared this night, with its storm, suspicious passengers, and a body in the laundry, would never end.

4

5 a.m. The ship was still rocking and rolling, but not with the same ferocity as it had when the storm first hit. Rachel planned to call a security team meeting for 8 a.m. for those not on duty in the CCTV monitoring office. CCTV monitoring was a vital part of the security team's work. Members watched screens covering almost every working part of the ship, including the bridge.

Rachel popped to the bridge briefly and saw that the senior officers were still occupied. She tried engineering, but that too was extremely busy. It wasn't the time to inform Peter Jenson about the body or quiz the engineers about what had happened to the power, but she hoped to do both before the security meeting.

She stepped into her office, a space that still felt foreign despite her frequent occupation. Each time she entered the room that had formerly been Jack

Waverley's office, she imagined his familiar face, welcoming but stern and always accompanied by the inevitable frown he used to greet her with. Now it was her domain. The space was expansive compared to her previous DI's cramped office, and she had to admit to enjoying its openness. Rachel had made it her own, replacing Waverley's huge desk with a sleek, more modern one. The shelves were lined with some of her go-to crime investigation books, as well as the procedural folders she had studied since taking up her new role. A photo of her and Carlos on their wedding day usually took pride of place on her desk, along with photos of her parents outside the vicarage where she'd grown up. There was also a photo of her brother, his partner, and her step-niece. These she had tucked safely away in her drawers after the storm warning.

A plush rug Rachel had picked up in Mumbai lined the floor beneath the coffee table in the more comfortable part of the office, where there were three easy chairs and a small sofa. These she hadn't replaced. A huge parlour palm that stood in the corner of that part of the office, adding a more homely appeal, lay on its side. As she picked it up and cleaned the mess, her mind wandered back to the many times she had sat in here with Jack Waverley, trying to convince him to listen to her theories, more often than not explaining why he had arrested the wrong person. Her lips curled upwards at the fond memories.

She had kept his espresso machine, which he'd left behind after he stopped drinking coffee. Rachel pressed a button and enjoyed listening to the gurgling sound as it prepared coffee. With the much-needed mug of coffee in her hand, Rachel settled in front of her desktop computer, secured in position so that it could withstand any weather.

After a quick glance at her wedding photo in the drawer, the first thing she did was call Carlos. He answered immediately.

"Thank God. Are you okay? I've been worried sick and following the storm. I tried to get—"

"Carlos, slow down. I'm fine, although I wouldn't want to experience another storm like that one."

"It's so good to hear your voice. How is everything?"

Talking with Carlos and catching up on news from home helped Rachel feel normal again. They spoke most days, but she usually waited for him to call her in case he was on a stakeout or something. His private investigation business kept him busy. Both their jobs helped them cope with the temporary separation her new position had created.

Once the call with Carlos ended, Rachel examined the images of the crime scene that Jason had uploaded remotely, scrolling through them one at a time. He had taken pictures of the woman's dead body from multiple angles, along with those of the area in and around the crime scene. Rachel zoomed in on the woman's face, noting smeared makeup and the look of surprise frozen on her features. Apart from that, the positioning of the body revealed nothing out of the ordinary. The poor woman's attacker had taken her completely by surprise.

Rachel read the detailed statement Ravanos had taken from the laundry attendant. Manuel Campos had worked for the cruise line for six years, a hard worker according to his manager, who supported a wife and two young children in San Salvador. Rachel recalled that the medical department's attendant, Raggie, hailed from El Salvador. It might be worth asking him if he knew Manuel, although the laundry worker was an unlikely suspect. The statement contained no fresh revelations. Manuel entered the laundry to check equipment before the start of his shift. The laundry had been evacuated during the worst of the storm over health and safety fears. Hefty containers filled with sheets, towels, and other laundry items ramming into someone could kill them, so it was a sensible precaution. The only useful piece of information regarding her investigation pertained to the clanging sound Manuel had heard, which had led her and Jason to the underfloor tunnel. Rachel was almost certain whoever had killed the mystery woman escaped via that tunnel on hearing Manuel enter.

"Who are you?" Rachel asked again while studying the photos of the attractive woman. "And why are you wearing an officer's uniform?" The only blessing from what Rachel could see was that the victim's death had been instantaneous, and, as Jason had pointed out, professional. The latter led to another dilemma. Why was she killed, and who killed her? Multiple questions ran through Rachel's tired head.

Before moving on, Rachel sipped her coffee, feeling the immediate caffeine boost that would help her concentrate. She studied the images of the body again. Other than the thumb marks on the back of the neck, there was no discolouration or contusions consistent with a fall. She couldn't be certain none were present without a naked examination. Rachel hadn't wished to strip the woman in the laundry and hadn't been wearing a forensic suit. She would leave that to Graham and his team before examining the body herself. Could it have been a robbery? No handbag, phone, or ID had been found at the scene. It wouldn't be the first time another passenger or crew member had lured a susceptible passenger into a trap, but in the middle of a raging storm? No. This had a distinct feel to it.

Rachel leaned into the back of the chair, her brain weighing up what she knew so far while finishing her coffee. The only thing she was certain of was that a young woman was dead, and it was up to her and her team to find out what had happened and apprehend the responsible person.

Remembering the micro-SD card nestled securely in an evidence bag in her pocket, Rachel donned gloves and removed it. Her fingers carefully placed the tiny card in an adapter before inserting it into the computer's port. She watched the screen while the virus scan ran its course. Once the card was deemed safe, her anticipation turned to despair. The data was locked behind a wall of encryption and password protection. Frustration rose in her chest. She sighed. Maybe the IT team could crack the code. But with no identifying information about the mysterious woman, their job wouldn't be easy.

Rachel's mind shifted to the evidence bags. She removed them from the secure safe only she and Jason had access to and placed them in a neat pile beside her computer. Inside one of them rested the smartwatch, a potential source of information. Still wearing gloves, she removed it from its bag. This part of the job she hated most, trawling through the fragments of someone else's life, hoping to uncover something crucial. It had always felt invasive to her, and still did, even after years of working in serious crime. The worst part was reading people's diaries. But this wasn't about morality; it was about justice. "Okay, time to see what you can tell me." She turned the device over in her hand, studying it for clues. An engraving would be nice. No such luck! There was nothing but the shiny black screen. The watch looked new.

Rachel pressed the power button on the side. The screen flickered to life. A four-digit passcode prompt appeared. Another roadblock in a frustrating case. It reinforced what she knew already; they would get nowhere until they knew who the woman was. She could try the standard 1-2-3-4, but that might make things harder for the IT team if she got locked out.

"We need a breakthrough."

The chair creaked as she got up and headed back to the coffee machine. After refilling her mug with fresh coffee and quickly draining it, Rachel decided there was nothing further to be gained by going through what she had in front of her. Replacing the smartwatch and micro-SD card back inside their evidence bags, she returned them to the safe and removed the latex gloves from her hands. Rachel ran her hands under the tap, enjoying the warmth and comfort of the soap and water. Time to go.

The next thing on her list was to get her head wound checked. If her hair was down, the dressing could be hidden, but that wasn't practical. She didn't want to be left with an ugly scar when her hair was tied back, either.

Rachel returned to her desk, logged out of the computer, and powered it down. Then she picked up the phone and dialled the security office.

"Hi Rosemary, it's Rachel. How's your night been?"

"Surprisingly quiet from a security perspective, but if you want to know about how I managed to stay on my feet, that's another story. All the injuries reported last night were due to falls rather than fights, which is a welcome change from the usual night shift. I'm glad we're seeing the back of that storm, though."

"Me too, along with five thousand others."

"Jason told me about the body in the laundry." Rachel had been happy to note that Rosemary Inglis was on the night shift. Her laid-back approach to life made the traumatic night sound almost comical.

"Then you'll know that Jason's uploaded photos of the victim discovered at 2 a.m. by Manuel Campos, a laundry worker. Mr Campos isn't triggering any red flags as far as I can see, but we'll need to check his story."

"And the dead woman?"

"She's triggering plenty of flags, but mostly about her identity and her clothing. Would you mind trawling through CCTV footage of all the laundry entry points, working backwards from 2 a.m. when the body was discovered?"

"No problem. I'll get right on it. Jason told me she was wearing an officer's uniform. That's weird."

"You could say that. And Rosemary?"

"Yes?"

"Check the footage of a hidden exit point 200 yards north of the wine cellar on the M1. You won't see it as an exit unless anybody appears to come out of the wall."

"I'm intrigued. Sounds like something you'd find in a Chronicles of Narnia book."

"Yep. But it's real enough; I'll explain later. I'll join you with coffee and doughnuts once I've been to the medical centre."

"Jason also told me about the bash to your head too," Rosemary said, chuckling.

"I'm going to have to have a chat with Jason about his blabbering. Are there no secrets on board this ship?"

"No, boss, there aren't."

Rachel laughed. "I'll bear that in mind. And the word 'boss' still sounds strange coming from you."

"I could always use 'ma'am.'"

"Please don't. I'll see you soon."

5

When Rachel strolled into the medical centre, the waiting room was unsurprisingly full. The faint scent of polish mingling with detergent hung in the air. Every clinic room was occupied. She paused, her gaze sweeping over the rows of occupied chairs. Rachel smiled at a few of the passengers, still in shock from the storm, as they waited to be seen. Some leaned against walls, while others sat hunched forward with heads bowed. All four of the centre's clinic rooms displayed red ENGAGED signs on the doors.

Rachel pushed through the heavy double doors leading into the infirmary. Here, it was more serene, although three beds were occupied. Patients lay between crisp white sheets, their faces marked with exhaustion, even in their slumber. A few shifted, murmuring in their sleep, but most remained still. Gentle snoring came from the bed at the end.

At the far end, Gwen Sumner, the chief nurse, stood by a bed checking charts, her brown hair tied back with not a strand out of place.

As Rachel approached, Gwen's eyebrows arched. It was enough to convey, I-know-about-the-body, to Rachel.

Rachel swallowed, trying not to giggle.

"Good morning, Chief. Are you looking for Nurse Bradshaw?" Staff always used formal titles when passengers were within hearing distance.

"No. But it looked busy out there, and I didn't want to take anyone away from their work."

"Yes. Busy for everyone." Again, the knowing look.

"Sarah suggested earlier that I get this checked." Rachel removed her cap, revealing the underlying dressing.

"Come through here." Gwen led the way into a side cubicle where a gleaming stainless-steel trolley was laid out with an array of medical supplies. There were bandages of every size, scissors and tweezers, along with antiseptic and ointments.

Gwen motioned for Rachel to take a seat on the padded chair while she stepped over to the sink and washed her hands. Then she slipped on a pair of latex gloves. "Okay. Let's see what we've got here." Gwen's eyes narrowed in concentration as she removed the dressing. Rachel winced as the adhesive tape pulled at her hair.

"Sorry about that. Sticky tape and hair don't make the best combination."

"I should have thought of that, but with all the ship's rolling while I applied it, I'm surprised the dressing landed on the wound at all."

Gwen grinned. "I assume this was the storm's doing."

"Yes, it threw me out of bed. I'm not sure what I hit, but once I managed to get into the bathroom, I tried a quick fix knowing how busy you'd all be."

"Was this before or after the blackout?"

"Before."

"You wouldn't know it looking at this glue." Gwen's Australian accent always came to the fore when she was being sarcastic.

Rachel smirked. "And there was I thinking I'd done a decent job."

"It's neat enough and stemmed the bleeding all right, so it shouldn't leave a nasty scar. Although I wouldn't normally recommend glue so close to the hairline, as long as you're careful with brushing, it should be okay. I can take away the excess where you got carried away, but I won't touch the wound. The repair's dry now, so you don't have to wear a dressing, but it might be better to have one on for a couple of days just to remind you there's a wound under there when you use a hairbrush."

Rachel grimaced at the imagery. "I can live with that."

Gwen removed a box of dressings from a store cupboard on the wall. "Are you okay with me shaving a little of your beautiful mane away? It'll make it less painful when changing the dressing. You can leave them off after a couple of days."

Rachel sighed. She wasn't a vain person, but her long blonde hair was her pride and joy. "Go ahead, if you must," she said.

Gwen gave her a sympathetic smile. "I'll only remove what's necessary."

"Thanks."

Gwen finished shaving and applied a fresh dressing. "These are shower-proof, but try not to soak them. Take this for spares." Gwen held out the almost full box.

"Anything else I should avoid?"

"Don't pick at the glue. It looks odd as it heals, but I'm sure you know all about that from your previous line of work." Gwen gave her a sly grin.

The senior nurse was right. Rachel had endured her fair share of injuries during her roles as a police officer, detective, amateur cruise ship sleuth, and now as chief of security. She had a few scars to prove it, but none were really ugly.

"Funny your first injury in an officer's uniform is accidental rather than due to your job."

"Hilarious," said Rachel.

"Do you have any other injuries to report?"

"Nothing to worry about. Just a bruised shoulder."

"Do you want me to take a look?"

They heard noises as someone else was being admitted to the infirmary. "I've got good movement. I'll let you know if I'm worried about it. About my job, has Graham had a chance to look at our body?"

Gwen shook her head. "Sorry, the entire team's been non-stop dealing with the aftermath. We've called in all our first aiders to help. They've been all over the ship since the storm stopped. I managed a brief look at the young woman when I undressed her for the refrigerator. There are no bruises other than those you've already seen – Jason sent the photos through, which support the theory of the death not being an accident. I would have expected more injuries if she'd been tossed onto that conveyor belt by a storm. Her landing was too convenient for it to be accidental. There's one interesting thing you should look at, though."

Rachel's interest piqued. "Oh?"

"You know the code. Have a peek at the right shoulder blade. It isn't the first time your mystery woman has been in the wars."

"Definitely the last, though."

"Sadly, yes. Why was she wearing an officer's uniform, and what was she doing in the laundry during the worst storm ever?"

"That's what I'd like to know. Our working theory is that she was meeting someone. It seems more likely than doing it for a prank. Rosemary's trawling CCTV as we speak. Did you notice any distinguishing marks?"

"Other than the old wound on the right shoulder, which she tried to disguise with a butterfly tattoo. It's a decent job, and if I hadn't looked closely, I'd have thought it was like those thousands of women her age have," said Gwen.

"Okay. Enough teasing. What caused whatever it was she was trying to hide?"

"I'm no expert, so I don't want to say. Graham will know."

"How old would you say she was?"

"From skin tone and eyes, thirty to thirty-five. And muscle tone suggests she was almost as fit as you."

"Interesting," said Rachel. "You don't recognise her? She couldn't be a new officer I haven't met?"

Gwen shook her head. "Nope. We see all the newbies for medicals, as you know, and you'd be introduced to senior officers. I agree with the others. She's not crew; the labels are wrong. At least it narrows it down to eight hundred women in the twenty-five to thirty-eight age bracket, allowing for a bit of latitude on my estimate, among the passengers. Do you have any other clues?"

Rachel scrunched her eyes, trying to focus. "A micro-SD card we found in an underfloor tunnel, but it's password protected and, I suspect, encrypted. It could also belong to anyone. There's also a smartwatch with a passcode I can't get into. As you've hinted at something that might help me. I'll see her on my way out?"

"I think I can trust you to go unaccompanied. She's in drawer one under the name Jane Doe."

"Very original," said Rachel.

Bernard appeared at the door. "Hi Rachel," he said, giving her a wide grin, but his eyes were tired as he looked at Gwen. "We've got a suspected ankle fracture. Do you want me to do the X-ray?"

"Have you got time? I'd better check on the rest of our inpatients."

"No problem, boss. Looks like we're going to have beds in the corridor at this rate."

Rachel's mind shot back to dreadful sights of hospital corridors in emergency departments in Leicester, where she had often been to interview victims and relatives.

"Not on my watch, we won't. I've put a call out for all the first aiders who aren't on duty elsewhere to help with injuries. Most people won't need admitting. Thank

God it happened in the middle of the night and not when the ship was in full flow. I'll see you later, Rachel."

"Thanks, Gwen," said Rachel.

On leaving the medical centre, she turned right, tapping in the key code to enter the morgue.

6

Rachel pulled open the refrigerated drawer containing Jane Doe. The soft mechanical whir of the mechanism echoed in the silence of the ship's morgue. When she'd first realised, as a passenger, that cruise ships had morgues, she'd been surprised. It made sense to her now. With thousands of passengers, including many elderly, sailing across vast oceans for weeks, sometimes months at a time, death was a statistical certainty. The morgue was in a quiet corner on deck two accessed via the medical centre, and was a necessary facility, albeit not one advertised in brochures. Most deaths aboard ship occurred from natural causes and didn't require the security team's involvement.

A white sheet covered the body, and as she pulled it back, the first thing she noticed was that the woman's eyelids had been closed. The face seemed more relaxed than when Rachel had last seen it. The woman, who must have been pretty in life, looked as though she might breathe at any moment. Rachel shivered, despite the temperature-controlled environment. Working in serious crime in England, Rachel had seen her fair share of bodies, but it didn't seem right when people died at sea. Perhaps it was the contrast between the holiday atmosphere above decks and this stark reminder of mortality.

Shaking such thoughts from her head, Rachel folded back the sheet, uncovering the torso. The bright light highlighted the woman's skin, making the muscle definition apparent. On close inspection, Rachel could see what Gwen meant by the athletic build.

Rachel removed the radio from her belt and changed the channel, the static crackling through the room. The morgue wasn't huge, but it had enough space for four refrigerated drawers, a basic examination table, and some equipment. Everything was secured against the ship's movement, which was perhaps as well, considering the storm they had just experienced.

Jason answered her call immediately.

"I was just about to call you to see if you'd got anything from the evidence," he said.

"Nothing. It's all passcode protected. I've got the items in my pocket to take to IT." Rachel absentmindedly patted the pocket containing the micro-SD and the smartwatch. "Look, I'm in the morgue. Gwen says there's a scar we need to look at, but I don't want to handle the body roughly, so I could do with your help. Plus, I've got a feeling I'm going to need your army expertise."

"Okay. I'm on my way."

"Wait a minute, Jason. Bring a fingerprinting kit with you, would you?"

"Why didn't I think of that?"

"Because you're not an ex-cop and it's not usually necessary," she said, laughing, though the sound felt out of place in the sombre room. "I'll make notes until you get here."

"Sure. I'm close to security supplies. I'll get what we need and be with you."

While waiting, Rachel inspected the front of the woman's body from head to toe. Her gloved fingers brushed back the light brown hair, searching for anything the killer might have left behind. Graham Bentley had already taken swabs, which would be sent away for DNA sampling as soon as they reached port. For now, they only had what was visible to the naked eye.

There was scarring over the right knee, indicating previous knee surgery. "You are a genuine mystery, Jane Doe," said Rachel, her voice almost a whisper.

"Talking to the dead. You might need to see a doctor for that." Jason's voice cut through Rachel's musings, making her start slightly. She hadn't heard him come in.

"What do you make of this?" Rachel covered the top half of the woman's body and pointed to the knee in question, grateful to have someone with her. Jason was always calm and a great support.

"She's had surgery. Dr Bentley would know more about that than me." He leaned closer, squinting at the scar tissue.

Rachel wondered if the chief medical officer would be happy to X-ray the knee of a dead person but doubted it would add anything to the investigation. The ship's medical facilities were designed for diagnosing and treating living passengers, not conducting forensic investigations, although Graham Bentley knew what samples to take following a suspicious death. "Let's roll her onto her side. It's the right scapula we're interested in, but we should check the body as best we can. Graham's too busy to do it just yet."

Between the two of them, they moved her body onto her side. The metal drawer creaked slightly under the shifting weight. Rachel could immediately see what Gwen had referred to: a scar beneath a butterfly tattoo.

Jason squinted again, something he did when thinking. "I'd say that's a Red Admiral."

"As much as I appreciate dark humour, Jason. Now isn't the time." The words came out sharper than she'd intended, the stress and lack of sleep taking their toll.

"Sorry, I only do that to ward off traumatic memories from the battlefield." His voice was quiet.

Rachel felt immediately sorry for her rebuke. She knew only too well, being married to a former soldier, how PTSD formed a part of their being. She cast him a sympathetic glance before speaking. "I take it the scar's from a bullet wound?"

"That's what it looks like." His fingers hovered over the scar without touching it. "A nine millimetre, I'd say."

"So we could be looking at a criminal or someone who's ex-military?"

"Could be either," said Jason. "I'm guessing private contractor, but I've no reason for saying that." His expression was troubled, and Rachel suspected he was recalling his past.

"We'll keep all three as options for now. Hold her still for me while I scan the rest of her." The rest of the examination revealed nothing. Rachel gave Jason the nod to let her roll onto her back.

"Shall I take the prints?"

"Yep. At least we should be able to rule out the criminal link if they come back clear." Rachel watched as Jason worked methodically, pressing the fingers and thumbs of each hand into the pads and rolling them from side to side on the required sheets before placing them inside a folder. She wondered about the woman's last moments. Had she known the danger she was in?

Rachel re-covered the body with the sheet and

pushed the drawer closed. It gave a soft thud as it locked in place. The nameplate would be Jane Doe until they discovered her true identity.

"What next, boss?" Jason's question drew her mind back to the present.

"I'll send those prints to my former DCI and ask him to be discreet. We really need to know what this woman was doing aboard this ship and whether she was working with someone." Rachel's mind was racing ahead to the next steps in the investigation.

"Other than her killer, you mean?"

"Yes," said Rachel. "I'm heading to see Rosemary now. I asked her to trawl the CCTV. That should tell us something. Can you let the rest of the team know we'll meet at 8 a.m., sharp, in my office?"

"Do you want them to know about her?" Jason's head motioned to the closed drawer.

Rachel rubbed her temple again. "Ouch. I've got to stop doing that." The pain from her earlier accident was still tender. "Do you think we should keep it between those who know already for now?"

"Until we know what we're up against, it might be worth it. A lot of newbies joined the team in Iceland."

Rachel weighed up what he'd said, baulking at the thought that one of their own might be involved in something like this, but Jason's suggestion made sense. "You're right. We don't want to scare them anyway. Tell

Ravanos to keep shtum, although I doubt our laundry man will keep it to himself, so we don't have too long."

"I'll get on with contacting them and track Manuel and his manager down – see what I can do," said Jason, handing Rachel the folder.

They left the morgue together before separating at the junction outside the medical centre. The corridor was quiet, most patients unaware of this part of the ship's existence. Above them, thousands of people were catching up on sleep and would soon forget about the storm that had shaken the ship to its core. They would be totally unaware a killer walked among them.

Rachel's head throbbed, but not from the wound this time. Could they really have a traitor among the crew? The thought chilled her more than the morgue's refrigerated air. On a ship, there was nowhere to run. The killer was trapped onboard too, and sooner or later, she would find them.

7

As Rachel entered the CCTV office with its multitude of monitors, she smiled when she saw Rosemary. The smile faded when she spotted Tamara Shutt, a recent addition to the team, in earnest conversation with her. They were hunched over a computer, but both turned to look at her.

She felt herself bristle. "I didn't know you were on duty, Tamara."

"I couldn't sleep, and to be honest, that storm scared me to death, Chief."

There was something about the new girl's overenthusiasm that got under Rachel's skin, an irritation she couldn't explain, as she wouldn't normally wish to snuff out a person's keenness. The annoyance left her feeling guilty. She placed the plate of doughnuts she'd collected from upstairs on the desk.

"Oh, thank you. Now my stomach's settled, I might eat one of those," said Rosemary. "Tamara's been helping me go through the CCTV."

Unlike Tamara, Rachel found Rosemary Inglis easy to get along with. Rosemary was a former Olympic white-water slalom competitor who Rachel had got to know when exercising her investigative skills as a passenger. Rosemary was open, helpful, loyal, and knew when to keep things to herself. "Have you found anything?"

"I've found our Jane Doe just before she entered the secure area." Tamara might irritate Rachel, but she had to admit her history of working in military intelligence would likely be useful in this case.

"The thing is, boss, I'd gone over that same footage numerous times and couldn't see her. Tamara found her in minutes." Rosemary eyed her new colleague with admiration, whereas Rachel found that fact concerning.

"Show me." The two women shifted their seats to allow Rachel space to pull a chair between them. Tamara played a section of video back. It showed the now-dead woman swiping an access card at the entrance to the laundry, but when they rolled the film further backwards, she wasn't in shot. It was as though she was a ghost, appearing from nowhere. Rachel felt her eyebrows knit together. Rosemary was nobody's fool, so how had she missed it? "How can that be?

Where was she before this bit?" And how the heck did she get hold of a ship's swipe card?

"That's the interesting part," said Tamara, her eyes lighting up with enthusiasm. "She, or someone else, seems to have used a video blocker."

"This might sound like a foolish question, but as I've never heard of such a thing, what is a video blocker?"

"It's brand new, state-of-the-art technology, only used by the military and almost impossible to detect. In the old days, people, especially thieves, doctored footage after it was recorded or used mirrors to pretend a space was empty while using a recording on a loop. That way, they could hide from live cameras, but it's fraught with difficulty. You've probably seen that sort of thing in films."

"And come across it in my old line of work, so what makes this technology different?"

"It's AI-generated and can make a person seem invisible."

Rachel reached for a doughnut, taking a large bite. She needed the sugar rush.

Recognising Rachel's confusion, Tamara went on. "It's really cool. Basically, you become a ghost to security cameras."

Rachel held her breath, weighing up the information. "Not so cool if it's in the hands of criminals on this ship. If she used such equipment, how did you find her?"

"The technology's advanced, but it's also new, and it has flaws. I'm not saying it is that, because I've never heard of it being used outside of specialist military research bases. But if it is, the blocker must have cut out for a minute."

"Or it could have been an old-fashioned glitch."

"True," Tamara admitted.

If the technology is top secret, what sort of clearance had Tamara Shutt had in the past? Rachel assumed from her CV that she was a low-level cybersecurity officer in the navy. Chomping on her doughnut, she took a coffee from Rosemary, who had boiled the kettle since she arrived. "Thanks."

"I don't know how I missed it. Tamara's much better at this sort of stuff than me. If advanced technology is being used on board, we need her expertise."

Tamara seemed to know her stuff, but Rachel wasn't buying the idea that Rosemary had missed the woman's presence and hadn't spotted the glitch or whatever it was. There was more to the scene than what they were seeing – or being shown, but she didn't have the expertise to challenge it. "Let's keep an open mind on the technology for now. Weird things happened during the storm from hell. I'm not ready to accept that we have top-notch military-grade technology in the hands of person or persons unknown." Rachel could have kicked herself for her scepticism. She sounded more like Waverley every day. Since taking on her new role, she understood how difficult it must have been for the security chief to shoulder the responsibility for the safety of over five thousand lives. She shook her head back into reality. "Do you see anyone follow her?"

"Unclear," said Rosemary. "The CCTV catches three separate incidents. Two are crewmen falling over not long after she entered the laundry. The woman entered the crew-only area and then the laundry when the storm was throwing its worst at us, and the power cuts out soon after. We see nothing else until the power comes back on." Rosemary ran the footage forward from when the power came back on; first, a man in blue overalls toppled into the door the woman had entered but then recovered and teetered off in another direction. The second person, an officer, had his back to the camera. Rachel didn't recognise him. He held onto the rail running along the wall but was eventually forced to let go and ended up on the other side of the corridor. His face and badge remained out of shot.

"Do either of you know that officer?"

They both shook their heads.

"Nobody enters that area before the blackout, but it doesn't mean to say they didn't go in there after," said Rosemary.

"Or they were using a video blocker," Tamara persisted.

"Or that," conceded Rachel. "We'll need to track that

crewman and the officer and speak to them. They might have seen something."

"I'll get onto that," said Tamara.

"Who's that?" The video footage was still playing, and Rachel saw a tallish woman with wavy hair hanging onto the laundry door.

"That's our celebrity chef, Belinda Marlow, most likely on her way to the kitchen to check her precious dishes haven't been destroyed," said Rosemary. "I'm surprised you haven't met her since she's been given behind-the-scenes access."

Rachel felt annoyance settling on her stomach, but for now, she said, "I've heard about her. She's hosting exclusive culinary events and a fundraising auction. I'm attending one tonight." Putting Belinda Marlow to one side for a moment, Rachel looked at the two officers. Why did a woman disguise herself as a senior officer and enter the laundry in the middle of that horrendous storm, and where did she get the swipe card?

"If she's got the technology to block video, she would have the ability to clone a swipe card," Tamara said.

"Let's take a step back and look into that. As I've said, I'm not ready to accept the video-blocking theory yet."

Tamara pouted, opening and closing her mouth. Rachel noticed Rosemary giving her colleague a warning shake of the head, and Tamara bit down whatever it was she was going to say. Rubbing her head, Rachel winced again as she accidentally touched the dressing.

"Is that sore?" asked Rosemary.

"It is, but it could have been worse. How come neither of you are injured?"

"I'm glad everything in here is bolted down, or the equipment would have been smashed to pieces. As it was, I clung on to a table leg to keep myself from hitting the deck."

Rosemary's muscular arms would have given her an advantage in that department, thought Rachel. Her canoe slalom history meant she was broad from the waist up, and she'd kept up her gym training. Rachel worked out regularly but was more into cardiovascular exercise than muscle building. She flashed Rosemary a friendly smile. "Let's hope we never hit another one like that while I'm here, or I might just change my mind about this job."

"Don't you dare."

"What's next?" Tamara interrupted.

"Can you use your expertise to find this woman among the passengers, working backwards from where she entered? Even if there is some technology we don't know about, I can't believe she, or someone else, was using it the whole time, especially if it's glitchy. What name comes up from the swipe card she used?"

Chapter 7

Rosemary tapped a few keys and then stared at Rachel, wide-eyed. "You will not like this, but it's registering as the chief of security!"

Rachel's hand reached for her lanyard. It was still in her pocket. "You're right. I don't like it. And it confirms this woman was no ordinary passenger. I want to know everywhere she went and everyone she spoke to, even if it was a simple hello. She might have been working with someone. We need her name." Rachel didn't want to have to search every stateroom on the ship, but she would if she had to.

"Yes, boss," said Rosemary.

"What about the M1?" Rachel asked Rosemary.

Rosemary cleared her throat, then grimaced. "We lose it at midnight. I sent one of our guys to check, and the cable had disconnected. It must have been the storm."

That seemed plausible but was yet another one of these horrible coincidences Rachel didn't like.

"Rosemary, Jason's contacting the team. We'll meet in my office at 8 a.m." Rachel finished her doughnut and stood up.

"Where are you going, boss?" Tamara asked.

"It's time I gave Captain Jenson an even bigger headache than the one I suspect he's got already. Then I'm going to get our tech team out of bed. I'll see you at eight unless you find anything important. Rosemary, can you join me outside for a minute?"

Rosemary eyed Rachel after closing the door. "What is it?"

"Something feels off. I'm not saying it is, but keep an eye on our new recruit, will you? Don't let her enthusiasm keep her from sharing, and make sure you know what she's doing."

"I think she just wants to impress you, Rachel."

"Maybe. But I'm not taking any chances." *As long as enthusiasm is all it is, I can live with it*, thought Rachel. Maybe that's what was irritating. Tamara Shutt was keen to impress, but if it wasn't kept under control, it could put her or the team in danger, especially if she didn't keep people in the loop. Her background in cybersecurity could well turn out to be a bonus, but she'd only been with the team for a couple of weeks. *A couple of weeks before we have a cyber meltdown,* thought Rachel, never a fan of coincidences. Or maybe she's just cleverer than you, her inner nemesis said.

"In which case, I'll defer to her superior knowledge," Rachel said out loud.

"Sorry?"

"Just thinking. By the way, who gave the celebrity chef behind-the-scenes access?"

"Foster." Rosemary looked worried. "He said he would clear it with you."

Clint Foster, I might have guessed, Rachel thought. One of Waverley's incompetent and lazy officers who thinks women belong in the kitchen. She had given him every opportunity to get onboard with the new hierarchy, but being a dinosaur, he couldn't accept it. Insubordination and endangering the security of this ship, she would not tolerate. "I'll see you at the meeting, but let me know if you find anything else I need to know about."

8

Rachel swiped her card to enter the bridge. Although people were moving a little quicker than normal, the atmosphere struck her as one of calm efficiency. The storm had been downgraded, but gigantic waves continued to crash outside, albeit with less intensity since daylight had appeared. The bridge officers seemed controlled and professional as they went about their work. Rachel's head wound throbbed beneath the dressing, probably due to the adrenaline that had kept her going for hours wearing off.

"Good morning, Rachel. How did you find your first major storm?" Captain Peter Jenson's familiar smile was wide, but the dark lines under his eyes, along with the slight strain around his mouth as it stretched, told her everything she needed to know. His normally pristine uniform showed subtle signs of the night's chaos, with a crooked epaulette and the tiniest coffee stain on one cuff.

"I was just coming to hand in my notice." Rachel matched his teasing tone with a smirk. The bridge's array of monitors cast a bluish glow, making Peter's – she would get used to calling him that one day – exhaustion more apparent.

His face changed, humour vanishing. "I hear you've got something to tell me. Why don't we go to my quarters now that things have settled down?" He gestured toward his private quarters. "Nicolas, you've got the bridge."

"Yes, sir." Nicolas Evans looked up from the navigation display, his fingers hovering over the electronic charts showing the ship, and more importantly, the storm's position.

The external sounds became muffled as they left the bridge, but Rachel could still feel the ship's subtle movements beneath her feet. "I heard horns earlier. What were they about?" Rachel asked, following Peter Jenson into his living quarters, a few yards from the bridge. The captain's personal space felt official but not minimalist; rather, it felt lived in. It comprised a large sitting room as well as private bedrooms. She'd been told that Nicolas Evans, who lived aboard with his family, had a cat in their quarters, but Peter's children were teenagers in school, so he only saw them during rare leave and school holidays when they joined the ship with his wife. She wondered if he missed his family as much as she missed Carlos.

"It's routine to sound warnings when aware that other ships are in the vicinity during a storm and visibility is low. Although most vessels have radar, one can't be too careful." A frown crossed his face. "Ours has never failed before. The most recent horns were a warning to a cargo ship that looked like it might veer off course, but it has since shifted out of our way." His eyes fixed on her injury. "I see you didn't escape unscathed."

Rachel's fingers automatically moved to the dressing, wincing as the throbbing increased. She could also feel her shoulder stiffening as the bruising made its presence known. "No, sir, I had a rude awakening. Was that the worst we're likely to come across?"

"Not the worst," Peter rubbed his temples. "But certainly the most unusual. I've got Bert and Aryna on their way to discuss what might have gone wrong, but Graham told me you have something else to report."

"I do." A knot formed in her stomach as reality set in. Rachel hadn't expected the captain to already know about the death, and it threw her off balance for reasons she couldn't understand.

"How much did Dr… erm… Graham, tell you?"

"Just that someone died from what looked like a fall, and you think it might not have been."

"Yes, sir, a woman in her thirties. That's about it in a nutshell."

"You can cut the 'sir' when we're in here, Rachel."

The captain's butler knocked on the door and entered with impeccable timing. Had he been listening at the door?

"What can I get you, sir?" The butler remained dressed in a black suit with a white shirt and tie, his wavy hair cropped short and efficient, a stark contrast to the chaos of the past few hours.

"Black coffee for me. How about you, Rachel?"

"Yes s..." Rachel caught herself, still adjusting to these more informal moments. "I mean, yes please, I'll have coffee as well, but with milk, no sugar."

When the door closed, Peter took a seat, motioning for her to do the same. She perused the family photos hung on the walls, which made the living quarters seem more homely. "How did they stay up?"

Peter followed her eyeline, smiling. "Special fixings. Nothing but a tsunami will shift those."

Rachel made a mental note to get the same for her photos.

"So how did this woman die? A fight got out of hand?" Peter Jenson leaned forward in his chair.

"I don't think so. It's an odd one..." She paused, gathering her thoughts.

"Odd seems to be the theme tonight."

The butler entered again, placing a tray with coffee and milk flasks, as well as a rack of toast. The china clinked as he put the tray down. "You know me well,

Hanz. Thank you. Tell Nicolas to send the others through when they arrive."

Peter buttered toast and suggested she join him. This domesticity was at odds with the seriousness of the situation she was about to reveal. But the scent of the toasted bread made Rachel's stomach groan, reminding her she hadn't eaten much at dinner the night before and had only had a doughnut since, which spiked her blood sugar but not for long enough. She buttered a couple of slices.

"Tell me what makes this woman's death odd?" The prompt brought her back to the task at hand.

Rachel inhaled before speaking. "The dead woman wore an officer's uniform and was found dead on the sheet press conveyor belt in the laundry. We believe her neck was deliberately broken." She stopped to let the words sink in, taking a sip of coffee. The warmth of the caffeinated drink brought instant relief.

Peter settled back in his chair. The coffee cup paused halfway to his lips. The soft cream leather creaked quietly. "From the way you've worded that, this woman wasn't an officer."

"No, we're certain she wasn't."

"That's something at least. I don't like anyone dying, but an officer... well..."

"Thus far, we don't know who she was or what she was doing down there. Nor do we know why she was wearing the uniform. I'm pretty certain there weren't any fancy-dress parties prior to the storm, although we'll check that with Nat. And another thing..." Outside, the wind made the walls groan like a living being.

The captain rubbed his tired eyes, nodding for her to continue. The lines in his face deepened.

"She used a chief of security swipe card to get inside the laundry." Rachel's right hand unconsciously touched her own card through her pocket.

"Yours?"

"No. I have mine, but there's a suggestion it might have been cloned." She hated admitting this. Security was her responsibility now, and someone had breached it.

"Has the card she used been retrieved?"

"Not yet, but mine's been reconfigured. She had no possessions other than a smartwatch, which we assume the killer didn't have time to remove."

Peter Jenson sighed. "What's your theory?"

Rachel considered her response. Since joining the ship as the chief security officer, she had come to appreciate Peter's leadership style. He'd welcomed her changes, giving her a free hand to update what she felt needed changing while remaining loyal to his departed security chief's legacy. He was also astute and knowledgeable, open to her methods, and his support had helped smooth the transition with most of her team. Some still clung to the old ways like barnacles to a hull and would prefer to meander through life without accepting new tasks or responsibilities. Others, like Tamara Shutt, were new in post and still in training. "It's difficult not to link the dead woman's presence with the ship-wide blackout just after she entered the laundry." She didn't mention the disconnection of CCTV on the M1.

"Okay. What do you think she was up to? The laundry is nowhere near any of our vital systems."

"I can only imagine she was meeting someone, a crew member. For good or nefarious reasons, I can't yet say." Rachel watched a muscle twitch in Peter's jaw.

"And the timely blackout prevents you from ascertaining who that meeting, if there was one, was with?"

"Not only that, but there's a small possibility she, or someone else, was using some sort of video-blocking device that's making it hard for us to track her movements before she entered the laundry." Rachel leaned forward slightly, noting how the captain's shoulders tensed. "Do you know more about this than I'm telling you?"

Peter poured himself another black coffee from one of the hot flasks. Rachel mirrored his actions.

"Not a word of this is to go out of this room. Do you understand?"

"Understood," said Rachel, her pulse rate increasing.

"If the others arrive, this conversation ends, and nobody but you, the medical team, and a few members of your team are to be told about this woman's death. If they find out, keep the details scant."

Rachel shifted in her seat, the leather squeaking against her uniform. "Okay. What's going on?"

Peter's eyes flicked towards his door, checking that they were still alone. He sighed heavily. "A few months ago, head office informed me of a potential cybersecurity threat. There's a flaw we don't know about that could allow a rogue agency – or even a rogue state to take control of our ships." He raised his hand as Rachel opened her mouth to speak. "It sounded like mumbo-jumbo to me, but the highest member of security at head office was sufficiently concerned to make every captain in the fleet aware of this possibility. We were told to look out for anomalies, reporting even the tiniest glitch up the chain. It's been difficult because I'm not allowed to utter a word about this to anyone, even my most senior officers, except to tell them we're operating on a theoretical risk basis. I'd thought it was a fantasy."

"Until now?" Rachel sipped her coffee, noting a red flush rising above Peter's collar.

"I didn't – and still don't – like the secrecy, but I was given no choice. I was going to tell you about this at the first sign of trouble; that time is now. But it has to stay between the two of us. The only other person you can involve, if you haven't already, is Tamara Shutt."

Rachel took a breath as the pieces clicked into place in her brain. "Things are beginning to make sense," she said, recalling Tamara's behaviour and why she'd appeared in the CCTV hub in the early hours. "I suspected something was off about her, but I imagined she just wasn't a team player. Who is she?"

"I knew you were smart, Rachel, and I wasn't convinced she'd escape your notice. Tamara Shutt is not ex-military. She's actually still in the military; a cybersecurity expert working undercover with permission from the cruise line at the highest level. There's an equivalent placement on every ship in our fleet. Each one of them comes highly recommended and has high clearance levels. She must not be exposed."

Rachel thought back to her conversation with Rosemary Inglis, mentally cataloguing everything she had said. Rosemary was trustworthy, but the more people who knew, the more dangerous it could become for Tamara. Secrets on board cruise ships had a way of spreading like oil on water. "I assume you weren't allowed to tell me about her real purpose either." Rachel felt a tad annoyed at being kept in the dark.

"Sorry. I'd like you to keep it that way. Don't let on that you've been informed, or she might not trust us. We need her on side. Behave as you have been, but use her skills to help you understand what happened tonight."

"I can do that." Rachel still had a niggle about Tamara Shutt, so she was happy to go along with Peter's plan. Not that she had any choice. On board the ship, the captain is to be obeyed.

A sharp knock at the door ended their conversation.

9

The knock was immediately followed by Hanz opening the door. "Nicolas asked me to show your guests through, Captain."

Peter Jenson motioned for him to let them in.

Aryna Petrova the chief engineer strode in first, her usually immaculate dark hair escaping its tight bun and creating a halo of frizz around her face. Her uniform was creased, likely from hours of crawling through access panels after the blackout. Behind her, Bert Holland's tall frame filled the doorway, his eyes red-rimmed from lack of sleep. Or something else; Rachel couldn't be sure.

"Coffee?" Peter gestured to the remaining cups on the tray.

"Please." Aryna's accent was more pronounced than usual, exposing her exhaustion. She bent over to pour herself a cup with precise movements, adding neither milk nor sugar. She didn't offer to pour for Bert. The IT head slumped into one of the leather chairs without speaking, waves of tension radiating from him. His tablet slipped from his fingers onto his lap, and he made no move to retrieve it. Rachel noticed his hands trembling slightly as he reached for the coffeepot.

"Can I get you anything else, Captain?" Hanz asked.

"No, thank you. Make sure we're not disturbed unless it's an emergency."

"Yes, Captain." Hanz left the room.

"Thanks for coming. I realise you've both had a horrendous night, but we need to discuss the power outage. Bert, I believe you've met our new chief of security, Rachel Jacobi-Prince."

Bert lifted his head but didn't offer his hand. "Yes, briefly. There are a lot of new people around."

Rachel tried to make friendly eye contact, but he was looking through her rather than at her. When she first joined the ship, Rachel had been introduced to all the senior officers but hadn't had much to do with Bert. All she knew was that he had been on leave and rejoined the ship in Iceland. Although Bert had been around when she took over the security team, it had been his deputy who had explained all the access systems, including giving her override permissions should she need them.

"I have preliminary findings about the power failure," said Aryna.

"Let's hear them," Peter said, his tone carefully neutral. Rachel recognised it as the one she was learning he used when dealing with potentially volatile situations.

Aryna remained standing, coffee in her hand and her spine rigid.

"Please sit down, Aryna," said Peter.

Aryna, another senior officer Rachel had been introduced to but didn't know well, was flicking her cat-green eyes between the captain and Rachel, as if fearing she might be placed under arrest at any moment. She sat in the fourth leather chair.

"The initial diagnostics show no mechanical failure. All systems were functioning normally until 01:00 hours when we experienced a total shutdown of primary and secondary power systems, and the backup generator didn't kick in." She paused, her jaw tightening. "There's no explanation for why this happened. IT told us this could never happen."

All eyes turned to Bert.

Bert finally looked up, his face etched with irritation. "If we could focus on the actual problem instead of subtle accusations..." He tapped his tablet screen awake. "A power surge from the lightning strike preceded the shutdown by exactly fifteen seconds. Our fail-safes dealt with it. What happened next was not normal."

Rachel leaned forward, intrigued. "What would be normal?"

"A cascading shutdown," Bert replied, some life returning to his voice as he focused on technical details. "Primary systems should move over to secondary power seamlessly. Instead…"

He trailed off, staring at something beyond the cabin wall.

"Instead, everything went dark at once, and we had a total system failure for twelve minutes and twenty-five seconds," Aryna finished for Bert, her expression softening slightly as she glanced at her colleague. "Like someone hit a giant off switch. But accessing those systems would require multiple security clearances and intimate knowledge of our infrastructure. Even you couldn't do it." She looked at Peter.

Rachel felt Peter's gaze on her but kept her expression neutral, remembering their earlier conversation. "Could the severity of the storm have triggered it?" she asked.

"Impossible," Aryna stated flatly. "Our systems are designed to handle much worse conditions than last night's. We've been through unavoidable категория пять."

"In English, please," said Peter.

"Apologies, Captain, category five hurricanes

without such problems. I know what you're thinking." She glared at Rachel.

"Nobody's thinking anything," Rachel replied, keeping her voice gentle. "We're just gathering information."

"No?" Aryna's laugh was sharp. "Because Russian engineer and mysterious power failure equals obvious conclusion, да?"

"Aryna," Peter's voice carried a note of warning. "Nobody is making accusations. You've worked with us long enough to know better."

Bert roused himself enough to add, "The timing is weird. The fifteen-second delay after the strike." His voice carried a bitter edge that seemed to go beyond professional frustration.

"Have you been able to trace the origin of the loss of power?" Peter asked, refilling his own coffee cup.

Aryna and Bert exchanged glances. "This is where it becomes complicated," Aryna said carefully. "The engineering logs and IT logs show multiple access points attempting to connect to our primary systems simultaneously. Like a coordinated attack, but..." She hesitated.

"But what?" Rachel prompted.

"But we can't determine the source, other than that the access signatures were internal," Bert cut in. "Whatever happened originated from somewhere on this ship and not from the lightning strike." His hand gripped his tablet tightly. "The initial signs were in the network diagnostics from yesterday's routine scan. I just didn't foresee it." He paused, his face clouding over.

Rachel watched as Peter leaned forward, concern clear in his expression. "Bert, you've been dealing with a lot lately. Nobody expects you to catch everything."

"My wife caught everything," Bert snapped, then immediately seemed to deflate. "Sorry. That was unprofessional."

An uncomfortable silence filled the room, broken only by the distant sound of the retreating storm and the ship's movement. Rachel used the moment to study the others. Peter's face showed compassion. Aryna's defensive posture had softened somewhat, and Bert seemed to retreat into himself.

"What's important now, what we need," Rachel said carefully, "is a systematic approach to tracking the access attempts. Aryna, can you show me where the power surge originated in terms of physical location?"

Aryna put her coffee cup back on its saucer and moved closer to the table, spreading out a digital blueprint of the ship on her tablet. "These are the points where we detected unusual activity." She highlighted several areas in red. "Engineering, bridge, medical bay, and..." she paused, frowning, "...for reasons I can't explain... the laundry."

Rachel kept her face carefully blank, though her pulse quickened. "The laundry seems a strange choice."

"Everything about it is strange," Bert muttered. "Even if the laundry was working at full power – which it wasn't – there's no way it could cause something like this to happen. The system architecture doesn't allow for this kind of coordinated access. It's as though..." He trailed off again, his thoughts seemingly elsewhere.

"As though what?" Peter prompted.

"Like someone knew exactly how our security protocols work," Aryna finished, her eyes narrowing. "Someone with intimate knowledge of our systems." She straightened her shoulders. "I know how this looks: Russian engineer, mysterious system failure. But I have dedicated my life to this company. For twelve years, I have served on cruise ships without a single problem."

"Nobody is accusing anyone," Rachel assured her, though she noted how Aryna's fingers nervously played with her security badge.

Peter took the cue. "We have to pool together to figure this out."

"What do you need from us?" Bert asked, attempting to focus. "It's a mystery."

"First, I need to know if this could happen again," Peter said, his tone making it clear this was his primary concern.

Aryna shook her head. "We hope not. Bert has implemented additional firewall protocols, and I've isolated critical systems. But..." She glanced at Bert.

"But we can't guarantee anything until we

understand how our security was bypassed in the first place," Bert finished. "We need time to do a full systems audit."

"How long will that take?" Peter asked.

"Minimum forty-eight hours," Aryna replied. "Possibly longer if we find more anomalies."

Rachel watched as Peter processed this information, knowing he was weighing the risks against their scheduled itinerary. "Do what you need to do," he finally said. "But I want regular updates. And everything stays between us for now. I don't want people thinking there's something strange going on. For now, it was just a surge from a lightning strike. You do what you do, and Rachel will investigate."

"Of course," Aryna nodded, some of the tension leaving her shoulders. "I should return to engineering. There are more diagnostics to run."

"I'll help," Bert said, standing slowly. "There's a pattern here somewhere. I just need to..." He pressed his fingers to his temples, leaving the thought unfinished.

As they prepared to leave, Rachel caught Peter's eye. The captain gave her a subtle nod, and she stayed put. The laundry's appearance on the list of affected systems couldn't be a coincidence, but she kept that thought to herself as she watched Aryna and Bert exit.

Although she had tried to sound reassuring, both Bert Holland and Aryna Petrova had to be ruled out as suspects. Rachel had a dead woman in the morgue, a compromised security system, and now evidence of a coordinated attack on the ship's infrastructure. The question was: how were they all connected, and who was responsible?

"What do you think?" Peter asked.

"There has to be an insider working with the dead woman."

"Agreed." Peter rubbed imaginary fluff from his sleeve. "I just hate to acknowledge it."

"Then I'll play the bad guy. What can you tell me about Aryna?"

"She's one of our success stories who has worked her way up to being the top engineer. What you're really asking me is whether there have been any warning signs that she might turn against us. The answer to that question is no. Aryna's parents moved to America when she was four years old. She holds dual US and Russian citizenship and is fluent in both languages, but as far as I'm aware, she has no living relatives in Russia."

"Why is she so defensive?"

"In the current political climate, Rachel, Russia is a pariah, although we try to keep that attitude away from this ship. As you know from previous cruises, we have many highly skilled Russian engineers, and I'd like to keep it that way."

"Don't worry. I don't carry any prejudices, but you

understand my need to check into her background and her contacts, both on and off the ship?"

"Just tread carefully."

"I will. Can you tell me more about Bert Holland? I knew he'd been on leave, and from what he said, his wife died recently."

"Yes. He rejoined us in Iceland after taking only two weeks' compassionate leave. I'm worried he came back too soon."

"What happened to his wife?"

"I don't know the details, other than she went into a private hospital in Switzerland for a routine operation, and things went wrong. He wasn't even there when she died. It happened so quickly."

"That explains his bitterness. Does he have support?"

"As you know, the ship now employs a counsellor. So far, he's refused to see her, but I'll have a word. I've asked his deputy to let me know if there are any concerns."

"Fritz Gruber, the guy who told me this could never happen."

"He was right until last night. It appears whatever this vulnerability is has been accessed. Nobody could foresee this situation."

"Except for whoever's behind it."

"Funnily enough, the one person Bert would have been able to speak to was Jack Waverley."

That explains why he has been less than friendly, thought Rachel. "Many people miss Waverley, me included," she said.

"He'd have hated this one on his plate. Technology was never really his thing, and he's enjoying retirement, if that's any consolation."

"Good." Although he hadn't been retired for that long.

Peter's eyes turned serious. "Find out who is behind this, Rachel, and whether it's linked to your dead woman. This is of the utmost importance and your top priority."

"We'll do everything we can," said Rachel.

"Now I'd better contact head office and see if they advise any further action."

"I've got a team meeting soon and have to work out a way of saying very little about the night's events."

Peter brushed back his hair again. "You have my sympathies. Keep me updated on your investigation. As soon as I've contacted head office, I'll make a reassuring announcement to the passengers."

10

The first thing Rachel did after leaving the bridge was phone Jason.

"You're using the phone. This must be private," he said.

"Can we delay the team meeting for a couple of hours? I want to send the prints away, and like you suggested, we're not to mention the body to anyone not already in the know."

"It makes sense. I assume you'll fill me in later."

"Yes, of course."

"I'll tell them ten o'clock. That gives them time to eat or whatever," said Jason.

"Thanks."

Rachel scanned the prints Jason had taken and sent them to her former DCI.

His reply came quickly, teasing that he knew she'd be begging for favours before long. Rachel didn't expect they would yield any leads, but anything was worth a try. She looked up when she heard someone entering her office.

"I thought I'd find you still working."

Rachel was pleased to see her best friend sashaying across the room.

"I bet you never entered like that when Waverley was here," Rachel couldn't suppress a giggle.

Sarah smirked. "You're so right. Although I would have liked to sometimes. Is it okay to say I still miss him a little?"

"It's absolutely fine. I'm still suffering from imposter syndrome and, quite honestly, would like his guidance right now. Are you off duty?"

Sarah exhaled a heavy breath. "Until evening surgery, then I'm on call. It's been all hands on deck, literally. We've been at it all night."

"Yeah, I saw Gwen about my bump, so you can relax about that at least. We're going to have a lot of tired crew today."

"And passengers," said Sarah.

"The medical centre was packed when I got my head checked."

Sarah smiled, her green eyes fighting tiredness. "Good to know you do as you're told sometimes."

"Gwen wasn't overly impressed with my repair, but she said it would do. Coffee?"

"I'll have herbal tea if you've got any. I'm going to get a few hours' sleep."

"I've only got raspberry and blackcurrant. I don't usually ask for herbal teas, but I could call down?"

"Raspberry and blackcurrant is fine. Leave the tea bag in the water, will you?"

Rachel got up and used hot water from a flask to prepare Sarah a drink while pouring a strong coffee for herself. She left Sarah's tea bag in the mug and placed the steaming hot drinks on the coffee table. She sat on the two-seater sofa from Waverley's tenure.

Sarah took a comfy armchair. "Thanks. I didn't get much to drink during the night." Sarah picked up the mug, swirling the tea bag around, using its tab as a spoon. Once finished, she removed it and placed it on a saucer before looking up. "As much as I love you, Rachel, I was looking for my husband."

"I'm gutted," she teased before realising Sarah was too tired to joke. "He's speaking to stateroom attendants, trying to find our dead passenger's room, beginning with the ones that have 'do not disturb' signs on their doors."

"I know I'm tired and not a member of the security team, but I wouldn't have thought that would be a useful exercise the day after a storm when hardly anyone slept."

"We have to start somewhere, but I get your point."

"How's the shoulder?"

Rachel rotated it automatically. "Not bad."

"So you still have no idea who the dead woman was or what she was doing in the laundry?"

Rachel felt her muscles tighten. "Nope. We'll drop off the samples Graham took when we're in port tomorrow, and I've sent prints to my old boss to see if we can ID her."

"Have you found out why the ship's failsafe didn't work?"

Rachel dropped her gaze, avoiding Sarah's trusting eyes. She shook her head.

"What are you not telling me?"

It had always been impossible to lie to her friend, but she was under orders. "Captain's orders, Sarah."

"Which means my husband will avoid speaking to me as well."

"I doubt it. If it's any consolation, the team isn't in the know on that one either, and I'd appreciate you keeping that information to yourself. I'm not comfortable with it. All I can say for now is that no-one knows for sure what caused the blackout. Plus, we don't yet know what the dead woman was doing in the laundry. Someone must have seen her, and if she was up to no good, I can't imagine she was working alone."

Sarah's eyes widened as she bit her lip, a telltale sign

since student days that she was stressing about something.

"What?"

Sarah shook her head. "Nothing. I thought for a moment... But no."

"Whatever it is, Sarah, tell me."

"Okay, but I don't think it's related."

Rachel leaned forward, the sleepiness that had been threatening to consume her, well and truly gone. "You've got good instincts, Sarah. Just tell me and let me decide."

"In the early hours, I think it might have been around 5 a.m. after I'd finished treating what seemed like hundreds of passengers, I found an injured man when I took a shortcut through the main restaurant."

"And?"

"He was a passenger, but I'm certain – well, almost certain – that he was heading for the M1 before I found him. He was injured, but I don't get why he ended up in the restaurant, especially not at the back close to the M1."

"Are you suggesting his injury didn't occur in the restaurant?" Rachel wasn't sure where this was going.

"Judging by the state of his clothing and a funny-shaped gash on his arm, I'm not sure. When I think about it, it was a ninety-degree L-shape. He said he was lost, and even though he was injured, he wouldn't come to the medical centre to be examined. Plus, he didn't want me to document it."

"What did you do?"

"What do you think?" Sarah folded her arms.

"You documented it."

"Of course I did. But I was so tired, I didn't explain to him I would need to follow him up. Ship's policy states we have to if injuries occur during a storm. I was going to see him later."

"So do you think he isn't insured and doesn't want a bill, or that he was up to something?"

"The insurance thought crossed my mind, but when I finally got back to the medical centre, I found out he's fully insured, so that can't be it. He seemed scared."

"A lot of people are terrified during storms. I was scared myself."

Sarah shook her head. "No. That wasn't it; he was fixated on the door to the M1."

"I don't suppose you searched him in case he was carrying a cloned officer's card?"

Sarah's jaw dropped. "Is that how the woman got into the laundry?"

Rachel nodded, her head throbbing at the reminder. "Not just any old card. The chief of security."

"Oh my."

"I've still got mine, yet the log showed it was me entering the laundry just before the lights went out. I can assure you I was otherwise engaged."

"So Alex could have had something similar."

"Who's Alex?"

"The passenger in the restaurant. I was called to a woman who'd passed out when he left me, so I was going to find out more about him, but I got distracted because Bernard needed a hand with a patient who needed a wrist plastered, and she was terrified about it."

Rachel's interest piqued. Two passengers straying close to the crew-only area. One dead and the other? She didn't know what the other was up to yet. "From your face, I'm guessing you don't believe Alex's story about him being lost."

Sarah now avoided eye contact, shaking her head. "I wasn't sure at the time, but he acted strange."

"I see what you're saying, but it's plausible that he was scared and got lost," Rachel suggested. *And we're all overreacting,* she thought.

"It is. I prescribed a lot of diazepam last night besides anti-sickness pills."

"I'm glad I had the injection, that's for sure. I tell you what, give me his full name and I'll check him out. Don't go to his room, just in case."

"His surname's on my laptop, which I left charging in Gwen's office. Can it wait?"

Rachel wasn't keen to wait, but she had plenty to do, and Sarah looked deadbeat. "Can't you remember?"

"Do you have any idea how many people I saw during and after the storm?" Sarah snapped.

"Sorry. It can wait until you've had your sleep." It might be nothing, she reasoned. Best not to poke the bear. Sarah could be difficult when she got overtired.

"It's Alex something. I think the surname began with an R because I had Alex Rider in my head. He looked a bit how I imagine an older Alex Rider to look. Not that he was old; late twenties, I would have said, also mixed Hispanic but educated in England from his accent."

"Thanks." That was a lot of information but useless without a surname.

"You know you can request access to my password from IT as chief of security, don't you?"

Rachel did know, but she didn't want to involve the IT team – especially not Bert Holland – in anything until she had had more time to digest the fact that the ship's systems could be compromised and that there might be an insider. She hadn't passed on the micro-SD card and smartwatch for that reason. Peter Jenson had assured her that the security team's records were doubly or triply encrypted and wouldn't be easy to break into. But then, weren't the ship's systems supposedly failsafe, and hadn't somebody used a clone of her ship-wide security card? Her only advantage was that whoever killed the passenger didn't know they were investigating it as murder, and she didn't want to alert them otherwise. She'd also asked Rosemary and Tamara to monitor her card use in case the person who took it tried to use it. It was a long shot, but worth a try. "I'm sure it's nothing, Sarah. I passed quite a few passengers wandering all over the place while attending my various meetings. The storm was disorientating. Your Alex could have strayed close to the M1 by mistake."

"Then why the interest in it?"

"Maybe curiosity. People pay for behind-the-scenes tours, remember?"

Sarah didn't seem convinced, but she was clearly glad at the let off. She drained her mug and stood up. "Tell Jason not to disturb me if you ever let him get some rest."

Rachel grinned. "Your husband's as much of a workaholic as I am, and I trust him to tell me when he's had enough. They're a good team... Mostly."

"Still having a few teething problems?" Sarah shot her a sympathetic glance before bending down to hug her.

"Nothing I can't handle," she replied.

As soon as Sarah was out of the door, Rachel moved back to her PC. She pulled up the passenger list and narrowed the surnames down to those beginning with R. Next, she typed in the name Alex. Ten could be excluded on account of gender, which left her with thirty names. She narrowed the list further to those in the twenty-five to thirty-five bracket. Now there were six. Three were travelling with children, and it seemed unlikely they would include the man she was looking for. That left three men's photos to check. Rachel sat back and wrapped her hands around the back of her head, her eyes fighting sleep. The ping of an email forced her to concentrate.

'Sorry, Rachel. No match on the criminal database. I can send it to Interpol, but it will take more time?'

Rachel replied, 'Yes, please. It's a long shot but might help. Thanks.'

11

Sarah pulled the covers over her head, her mind a whirlwind of thoughts that refused to let her sleep. The source of her confusion was the conversation with Rachel about Alex, the man she had briefly examined in the restaurant. The more she thought about his behaviour, the more she wondered what he had been up to and whether he had lied about getting lost. Frustration boiled over as she threw back the sheets. "This is impossible."

She sat up, caught between the desire to dive back under the covers and the urge to pursue the truth. Finally, she swung her legs out of bed, dragged her reluctant body into the shower, and dressed in a fresh set of scrubs. She wasn't due on shift until that evening but felt compelled to act. If she was going to pursue this, she needed to do it officially, or at least give that illusion.

The medical centre on deck two was all locked up, as morning surgery wasn't starting for another hour. Sarah used her pass to let herself in, avoiding the doors to the infirmary, where a passenger had been admitted for twelve hours to monitor for concussion. She stepped inside Gwen's office, feeling guilty about sneaking around. Her laptop was where she'd left it and was now fully charged. After opening the lid and pressing the start button, it fired into life. Sarah typed in her password. Tracking her consultation log made it easy to find the man she sought.

"Alex Reyes. I remember now. Where are you? Room 8892."

Sarah didn't want to put out a ship-wide call for Rachel, so she dialled her phone number, her heart sinking as it went straight to voicemail.

"Hi, you've got through to Rachel. Please leave a message and I'll get back to you when I pick this up."

"Rachel? It's Sarah. I couldn't sleep. The man I treated is called Alex Reyes; he's in 8892. He told me his stateroom was on deck fourteen, so he was lying about that. I'm heading up to his room now. I'll drop by your office once I've seen him."

Sarah closed her laptop and unplugged it from the wall before stealthily leaving the office.

When she arrived on deck eight, she noticed a

multitude of trays on the floor outside the stateroom doors. It appeared many people had taken advantage of room service once the storm subsided and were now catching naps. The stateroom attendants were attending to the rooms belonging to the more seasoned passengers who had left for breakfast. She didn't disturb them from their work and walked the length of the deck on the starboard side until she reached the room she was looking for. There was no tray outside and no sign on the door. Sarah knocked. No reply.

She knocked again.

Still no reply.

"Mr Reyes?" Sarah tried calling and knocking. The stateroom attendants were at the far end of the corridor, so she couldn't ask them.

Making a split-second decision, Sarah swiped the door with her universal door pass until it clicked. Turning the handle, she stepped inside, calling out again. "Mr Reyes? It's Sarah Bradshaw, the nurse who treated you during the night." The room was in darkness, with the heavy drapes covering the balcony windows. Sarah tiptoed inside in case he was in a deep sleep. Using her phone's torch as a light, she could see that the bed was unmade, but nobody was in it. Sarah reached for the light switch but was pulled roughly backwards, a hand clamped over her mouth. She tried to speak, but his grip was suffocating. In a swift motion, he twisted her arms and secured them in front of her with a plastic restrainer, forcing her into a chair. The room fell into an eerie silence as he switched on the light and locked the door, the click echoing ominously in the dimly lit space.

"What are you doing here?" Alex leaned over her, snarling through gritted teeth. His hands pressed down on her shoulders.

Gasping for air, Sarah's heart raced as she struggled to find her words. "I - I—"

Alex's dark eyes were wild. Through fear or malice, she couldn't work out. "I asked what you're doing here?"

"I came to check on you after your injury," she said between breaths, her voice strained, "and to check you were covered for tetanus because of the gash on your arm."

Alex's hand gripped his arm momentarily. A sweatshirt covered it. He had changed into a beige tracksuit and had replaced his smart shoes with black trainers. His eyes bore into hers, his expression unreadable. "I don't believe you," he spat out, his voice laced with venom.

Frustration and fear mingled in Sarah's mind as she fought to keep her composure. "Look. We have to record all consultations." Sarah's heart raced, but she summoned up years of expertise dealing with patients having mental meltdowns so as not to escalate the precarious position she found herself in.

"I said I don't believe you. Who sent you?"

"What are you talking about? No-one sent me. But if you don't untie me, my colleagues will be here with a security team."

"You're bluffing. Where's Eleanor? What have you done with her?" Alex was pacing the room like a coiled spring. He could pounce at any moment.

"Alex, you need to listen to me. I'm a nurse on board this ship, just doing my job. I don't know what you're afraid of or who Eleanor is, but please untie me. Perhaps I can help you find her."

Alex stopped pacing. His eyes met hers. "Why did you come in here?"

"I'll explain it if you take some deep breaths and sit down for a minute."

He pulled the other armchair next to her. His eyes were frantic, but he was inhaling and exhaling deep breaths as he'd done when she found him in the restaurant. "I don't want to hurt anyone."

"Well, that's a relief because I'm not here to cause trouble," Sarah modulated her tone, keeping her voice steady. "So please untie me."

Alex's gaze softened slightly. Uncertainty crossed his face. "Why did you sneak into my room?" he demanded, his voice shaky.

"Tell me about Eleanor. Is she a friend?"

"Colleague."

"What does she look like?"

Alex sprang from the chair like an unpredictable

predator, bearing down on her again. "You tell me, seeing as you have something to do with her disappearance."

"I've had nothing to do with anyone's disappearance, but a few hours before I met you this morning, a crewman discovered a badly injured young woman in the crew laundry. I was called along with the chief medical officer to tend to her."

Alex sat in his chair again. "Eleanor?"

Sarah's mind raced. She couldn't reveal suspicions of murder, but she had to keep him talking.

"We don't know her name. Show me a photo of your friend and I'll tell you if it was her."

"I don't have one… we… I told you she's a colleague."

"Mid-thirties, light brown hair, blue eyes?"

Alex rubbed a hand through his hair. "That sounds like her. Is she okay?"

Sarah's frown deepened as she considered her next words. What she said could shatter or salvage this volatile encounter. "I'm afraid not."

Alex became more agitated, springing up from the chair and pacing again. "This can't be happening. I-I don't know whether to believe you. You'll have to stay here until we dock tomorrow."

A lump rose in her throat as she swallowed hard. "Don't be ridiculous, I'm on duty in a few hours. People will look for me."

Alex yanked open the heavy drapes and stared at

the churning blue ocean, his mind clearly engaged in grim thoughts. Whatever he was contemplating wasn't good.

"What were you really doing when I found you this morning?" She had to keep him talking, silently praying that Rachel had got her message. Please, Rachel, don't be asleep.

"I was looking for Eleanor."

"Near the crew-only area. Why did you think she was there?"

Alex stepped away from the window, his pacing erratic again, panic ignited in his eyes. He was teetering on the brink. "Was it you she was meeting? Was it a trap?" he asked.

"I don't know what you're talking about. I spent most of the night patching up passengers and crew with injuries sustained during and after the storm. You saw me. Don't you know who your colleague was meeting?"

He rubbed a frantic hand across his cheek. "Enough! Be quiet for a minute – I need to think."

Sarah was happy to oblige because she needed to think too. Her pulse hammered in her ears as she scanned the room for something – anything – that could release her bound hands. A pair of nail clippers lay within reach. As soon as Alex turned his back, pacing towards the door, she reached out to seize the clippers. But her sudden movement knocked over the kettle. Alex whipped around, his eyes wild.

"Why did you do that?" he said, lunging forward. Sarah dodged him. In his frantic charge, Alex collided with the coffee table, smacking his shin painfully. He cursed.

Frantically, Sarah dashed to the door and unlocked it, only to be yanked back moments before reaching for the handle. "Alex. You need to stop this. Whatever you have in mind is not right." Sarah struggled to breathe, her heart racing at a rate that made her feel dizzy. Fear was making her freeze.

"How do I know I can trust you?"

"The chief of security is my best friend. I promise we'll help you."

Alex loosened his grip on her. She could almost hear his brain weighing up what she'd said.

"Okay." He cut the ties binding her hands.

"Thank you." As she headed for the door, the ship keeled. Sarah reached out to steady herself, but her arm was jarred violently, and she tumbled over. Searing pain exploded through her shoulder, causing her to scream. Alex rushed towards her, but he didn't get there in time. She hit the floor. Her head struck something sharp; the world blurred. She closed her eyes when she felt his hand on her neck.

Jason, I'm sorry.

12

The first two Alexes turned out to be dead ends. Sarah had said the man she met was mixed Hispanic, but these two were blonde and fair-skinned. Rachel was tired and hungry when her radio crackled to life.

"Rachel, it's Jason. Have you seen Sarah? She left a note saying she was doing something for you."

"What? No. When I saw her, she was going for a nap. Have you tried your room?"

"She's not here." Jason's voice shook.

"Hang on a minute, I'll check my phone." Rachel's phone had died, so she had put it into aeroplane mode to charge quicker. Her heart sank as she listened to the message. "Jason. Stateroom 8892. ASAP!" Rachel ran from the bow to the stern in minutes and took the stairs, as the lift areas were busy with passengers. A few gave her startled stares as she ran past them, but she wasn't stopping.

When she arrived outside the stateroom, she saw Jason further away, running towards her. She didn't wait. She swiped her card to unlock the door. A man, presumably Alex Reyes, was leaning over Sarah, who was lying on the floor. His eyes were terrified when he looked up.

"I think she's—"

Rachel felt rage like she had never experienced when she saw her lifelong friend lying on the floor. "Step away," she shouted, using her palm to strike his nose, sending him flying backwards. Her heart pounded at the sight of blood on the floor. Her fingers trembled as she felt Sarah's neck for a pulse.

Jason burst into the room, his eyes desperate at seeing his wife on the floor. He crumpled to his knees. "No. Please God, no."

"She's alive, Jason." Rachel called for an emergency medical team. "Stay with her while I deal with him."

Jason's eyes moved to the man getting up off the floor, and Rachel recognised in his eyes the same rage she felt and was still struggling to quell.

"If she dies..." Jason growled, but when Sarah moaned, his attention shifted to her. "It's okay, darling. I'm here." He leaned over and kissed her gently on the cheek, tears rolling down his cheeks.

Chapter 12

"Alex?"

"Don't worry. We've got him."

Rachel felt tears stinging the back of her eyes as she roughly handcuffed Alex Reyes' arms behind his back. His nose was bleeding where she'd hit him, but otherwise he looked like a man in shock.

Sarah jabbed her finger into Jason's chest while also looking at Rachel. "What took you so long?"

Jason couldn't speak; he just kissed her again. Graham Bentley and Bernard arrived, followed by Gwen.

"What happened?" Graham asked as he opened his medical bag.

"I'm sorry," Alex Reyes continued his sobbing.

Graham and Bernard assessed Sarah before turning her over to check where the blood was coming from. She had a gash at the nape of her neck.

"Ouch," said Bernard, grimacing. "Good thing it's not serious."

Bernard's humour broke the tension. "I'd be happy to swap places," said Sarah, forcing a smile.

"No thanks. I don't mind other people's blood, but I faint at the sight of my own," said Bernard, already opening his medical bag and reaching inside.

"She's going to be fine." Gwen squeezed Jason's hand before heading towards Rachel and Alex. "Let me look at that."

Rachel stepped aside to allow Gwen to treat Alex's nosebleed, which didn't take long.

Bernard brought in a stretcher, which he must have left in the corridor. Sarah argued, "That won't be necessary."

"I decide what's necessary," said Graham firmly, although the twinkle in his eye reassured Rachel that he agreed with the senior nurse's assessment that Sarah would be all right.

"Fine," said Sarah, allowing the medics to lift her onto the trolley. Gwen returned to assist her colleagues. As the team started out of the door with Sarah on the trolley, she asked them to stop and looked at Rachel. "I think your dead woman's name is Eleanor. Ask Alex."

"Eleanor's dead?" Alex leaned forward, his eyes filled with fear.

"You go," Rachel said to Jason. "I've got this."

"Thanks. I'll be in touch."

"There's really no need," Sarah protested.

"If this patient gives us any more trouble, Doctor, I suggest we sedate her," said Bernard, cackling.

"Stay with her," said Rachel, walking over to Jason. She lowered her voice. "Until we know what's going on, we need to keep this incident among as few people as possible."

"I take it you believe it's related to our Jane Doe?"

"You heard Sarah, I think it is," she said. "Swear the medics to silence about what happened, please."

"Jason! The lift's here," Gwen called.

After Jason left, Rachel took a seat next to her prisoner. "I'm Rachel Jacobi-Prince, chief of security. I take it you are Alex Reyes?"

Alex's eyes moved from Rachel to the floor. "Your friend said you would help me."

"Let's establish first that we are talking about the same person." Rachel brought up a photo of the dead body on her phone and showed it to Alex.

His eyes studied the image, then he nodded. "That's Eleanor."

"Okay, so who was Eleanor?" Rachel asked.

"I can't tell you. How do I know you're not in on it?"

"You have to trust someone, and as you've just hurt one of our best nurses and my best friend, I suggest you talk to me before I throw you in the brig."

"Are you serious?"

Rachel was struggling to control her temper. This man could have killed her best friend if Jason hadn't called. She inhaled deeply, exhaling slowly. "We take violence against staff extremely seriously, Mr Reyes. And we take criminal activity against our cruise ships just as seriously. You are looking at charges of attempted murder and industrial espionage at the very least, so I suggest you talk to me, beginning with Eleanor. Was she sent to break our systems?"

"No. And I didn't hurt your friend. Eleanor wasn't a criminal!"

Alex's eyes darted around the room, his shoulders slumping. He ran a hand through his wavy black hair.

"From where I'm sitting, you attacked an officer on board this ship, and your friend Eleanor was a criminal until proven otherwise," Rachel said.

"Look," he began, his voice defeated, "I promise I didn't hurt your friend. She came in here and I thought she was working for whoever took Eleanor. I zip-tied her, but she told me... she convinced me that she and you, would help me."

"You just happened to be carrying zip ties with you," said Rachel.

"They were Eleanor's. She said I might need them."

Rachel felt her eyebrow raise. "So who was Eleanor?"

"She was my mentor, my boss in this... operation." He paused.

Rachel leaned forward, her expression neutral but attentive. "Go on," she urged, sensing that Alex was on the verge of telling her what she needed to know.

Alex took a deep breath, his warm brown eyes meeting Rachel's gaze. "Eleanor worked for the British government," he said.

"Which department?"

"MI6." He took a handkerchief from his pocket and dabbed his nose.

"And you?"

Alex shook his head. "I was her security blanket. A

complete outsider. Eleanor wasn't big on trust, so she recruited me privately. I'm a hacker, that's all."

Rachel rubbed her head, trying to process what she was hearing through the tiredness threatening to overwhelm her. "What's her full name and what was she doing on board the *Coral Queen*?"

"Eleanor Brodie. She was a brilliant cybersecurity specialist, one of the best in the field. Her expertise was in detecting and preventing cyber terrorism."

Rachel's eyebrows shot up, but she remained silent, nodding for Alex to continue.

"She was assigned to this cruise ship because MI6 had intelligence suggesting that a sophisticated cyber-attack was being planned."

"The target?"

"The entire fleet of luxury liners owned by your company." Alex's voice grew stronger as he spoke, his professional demeanour slowly replacing his earlier distress.

"Where's the weakness?"

"I don't know. Eleanor thought she'd discovered a complex infiltration system embedded in the *Coral Queen*'s infrastructure. It was unlike anything she'd seen before – a masterpiece of malicious code, woven into the ship's systems. She believed it was the work of a state-sponsored cyber unit, though she couldn't pinpoint which one."

Rachel leaned forward, her fatigue momentarily

forgotten. "What kind of infiltration are we talking about?"

Alex's eyes lit up. "It's brilliant, really. The code lies dormant, undetectable by conventional security measures. But once activated, it has the potential to take control of critical ship functions: navigation, communications, even life support systems."

"How did she know all this?"

He paused, before saying, "There's a mole on board. Eleanor was close to cracking the case. She felt she could isolate part of the code, which is what I thought she was doing when the blackout happened. But then..." His voice trailed off, emotion taking over.

Rachel felt a chill run down her spine. "The blackout wasn't her test, was it?"

Alex shrugged. "I'm not sure. Eleanor might have taken advantage of the storm to trigger it deliberately, trying to force the dormant code to reveal itself. But if she did, something went wrong. Could her death have been an accident?"

Rachel shook her head. "Do you know who the mole is?"

"No. Everything she did was kept separate so that nobody could get the full picture."

"But you knew she had a meeting last night?"

"Yes. I told her not to risk it during the storm, but she said she had to, and the storm would provide the perfect cover for what she wanted to do."

"Would she have carried anything on her person that would be useful to her killer?"

Alex shook his head. "Only decoys. If they took what she had on her person, it would lead them down a blind alley."

Rachel sighed. "That's something, at least."

"Are you sure she was murdered?"

"I'm sorry," said Rachel. "Someone broke her neck."

The fear in Alex's eyes seemed genuine. "I wouldn't have taken this job on if I'd known. Eleanor seemed invincible."

"We all are. Until we're not. Now tell me, Alex Reyes. Were you going to kill my friend?"

"No. Ask her. We were coming to see you when a rogue wave hit and she fell. When you came in, I was checking for a pulse and was about to call the emergency team. I'm not a murderer, but I was terrified when she turned up in my room. Ask her."

"Don't worry. I will."

"Are you still going to throw me into your brig?"

"I'm thinking about it. First, tell me this: Were you frightened because Eleanor believed there was an insider on board working with this rogue state?"

Alex studied the floor. "It's someone high up. It could even be you."

"You might struggle to believe this, Alex, but it's not me, and it's not anyone from the medical team. I can vouch for all of them."

"What about your team?"

"Sarah's husband Jason is ex-military, so don't expect him to be too friendly towards you. Also, if his wife doesn't corroborate your story, I wouldn't want to be in your position."

"Call him."

Rachel radioed Jason. The tone in his voice was positive. "She's going to be okay. Graham wants to monitor her for now, but she's insisting on being discharged. Do you need me?"

"Not for now. Did Sarah tell you what happened?"

"I was about to let you know. She said Reyes was terrified, but he didn't hurt her. It was a fall. Is it okay if I stay with her after she's discharged? Otherwise, Graham won't let her leave the infirmary. I've asked him to wait until after our team meeting."

"Of course it's okay. And thanks, Jason." Rachel ended the call.

"Well?" Alex looked at her.

"It seems you are in the clear on that front, but you and your colleague should have come to me."

"That was never going to happen."

"At least you're honest. I need to keep last night's incident and your mentor's death as quiet as possible until I figure out what's going on."

"I can help."

Rachel came to a decision and removed his

handcuffs. "We'll see about that. You are to stay in your room until I tell you otherwise. In the meantime, save me some time and give me Eleanor's stateroom number."

13

Rachel used her universal swipe card to open Eleanor Brodie's stateroom, half expecting that whoever killed her would have ransacked it. Thankfully, that wasn't the case, which meant Eleanor had been discreet enough not to tell anyone her room number. She stepped cautiously inside, checking the immediate corridor and bathroom first. There was nothing out of the ordinary in either, so she proceeded into the main room.

The bed hadn't been slept in, and the rest of the room suggested an organised mind: no dirty clothes on the bed or hanging over chairs, no papers strewn across the coffee table, and the mugs and kettle were clean as though they hadn't been used. All this indicated that the occupant was either exceptionally tidy or exceptionally careful. The stateroom attendant wouldn't have been inside because the 'do not disturb' sign on the door prohibited it. The room was exactly how Eleanor must have liked it.

Rachel scanned it from top to bottom, trying to get a feel for the former occupant, but other than the possibility of her having OCD, nothing stood out. She headed to the safe and used her override code, thankful that she no longer had to work out entry codes as she had when investigating as an unofficial sleuth. After donning a pair of plastic gloves, she removed the contents of the safe. Nothing unusual, just currency, jewellery, and what she presumed were house keys and a car fob. Rachel checked the passport; it was Eleanor's.

Rachel bagged the passport and the contents of the safe before closing it again. She moved to the wardrobe, frowning when she found three different cruise ship uniforms on hangers: one junior officer's uniform, a kitchen worker's outfit, and engineering overalls. Badges and false names containing Eleanor's photo were pinned to each. If it wasn't for the internally incorrect labels that Sarah and Graham had mentioned – something no-one would check – the clothing was perfect. Eleanor could easily pass as one of the ship's crew. Rachel removed the badges and added them to her evidence bag, frustrated. She couldn't believe how easy it was for someone to wander around the ship posing as crew. The wardrobe also contained the more expected passenger clothes, evening dresses and the like.

Next, Rachel checked the bedside tables and drawers. Inside the top drawer were tickets for shore visits and one for the VIP dinner events, the first starting tonight. She stared at it. "The same chef who has been given permission to enter the kitchens willy-nilly, without my permission, is attracting a member of the security services to one of her dinners." On Rachel's ever-growing to-do list was a private word with Clint Foster.

A rap on the door disturbed Rachel's musings. She quickly bagged Eleanor's tickets and passes before answering.

Rachel looked down to see a woman of about five feet, five inches, with straight grey hair resting on her shoulders. She wore a pale blue trouser suit and had bright green twinkly eyes. She wasn't wearing makeup. Her bronzed skin hinted she might be a sun lover. The woman looked up at Rachel, producing a pair of reading glasses from nowhere and scrutinising her badge.

"Chief of Security? I'm impressed." She spoke with a southern Texas drawl. "Good morning, Miss... oh, I see it's Mrs Jacobi-Prince." The woman's eyes were now on Rachel's wedding ring.

"Good morning," Rachel said, smiling. "Is there something I can do for you, Ms...?" Rachel had noticed the absence of a wedding ring when the woman examined her badge.

Not giving her name, the woman said, "I'm looking for Eleanor Brodie. She didn't come home last night, and with the storm and all?" She spoke quickly. "I thought she might have gone overboard; I mean, that storm was something dreadful, and let me tell you, I've experienced some storms in my time. You didn't escape unscathed yourself, I see."

Rachel's hand automatically moved to the dressing on her head, impressed by the manic woman's observation skills.

"I'm certain she didn't come back to her room last night. I heard her go out in the early hours and wondered if she was feeling seasick."

"Well," said Rachel, unsure of what to say.

The woman in front of her continued, "But I always knew you'd catch her eventually."

Now Rachel's interest was piqued. "What do you mean?" she asked.

"My guess is Eleanor Brodie wasn't feeling sick at all and was up to no good. Did you arrest her?"

Rachel was totally confused and tired. Her brain was struggling to keep up and working slower than usual. "What makes you think I would arrest her?" she asked.

"Well, you see, I met her on another cruise about nine months ago." The woman leaned in closer, lowering her voice. "There was a suspicious death on that sailing. A man went overboard, and I'm convinced it had something to do with her."

Rachel was all ears but noticed that people had started to emerge from their rooms, and the stateroom attendants were getting closer, carrying out their morning chores. She didn't want to have this conversation in the corridor, nor did she want to invite the woman inside Eleanor Brodie's room.

"Would you like to have a chat about this?" said Rachel. "Why don't I join you in your room?"

"Oh no, dear. We must chat, but let's do it in a nice place. How about Creams?"

Rachel couldn't help grinning. Creams was her favourite place, as well as that of Sarah and her good friend, Lady Marjorie Snellthorpe. It was a place she had often frequented as a passenger. This woman reminded her of a slightly younger Marjorie, albeit with an American accent.

"Creams it is, then," said Rachel with a smile.

"I'll just collect my handbag," the woman said. Rachel closed Eleanor's door, leaving the 'Do Not Disturb' sign in place, and waited for the mystery passenger to come out of the room next door. Rachel checked the name label: Charlotte Kieft.

When Charlotte emerged, they began the walk along the corridor. The woman was in her late seventies but had a spritely walk.

"She pretended not to know me, you know," she

said, not pausing for a breath. "But I knew it was her. I'm not in my dotage yet. I tried to speak to her, but she blanked me. It was odd, and I thought perhaps I was mistaken, but when I checked the name outside her door wearing my trusty spectacles, I could see it was her. So, have you arrested her?"

They had arrived at the lifts, and Rachel pressed the down button. "Let's discuss it over coffee, Ms Kieft."

"Ah, you're clever. You did the same thing as me. Please call me Charlotte. I know I don't sound Dutch, and I'm not, but my father was, and for some reason they called me Charlotte – an English name, even though we lived in Texas. I've lived there all my life; although, to be honest, I spend as much time cruising as I do on the ranch these days."

Rachel's eyes widened. She has a ranch! She didn't think she'd ever met anyone who owned a ranch. Rachel liked this chatterbox of a woman, despite her obvious desire to gossip, so she'd need to be careful. Behind the talkative exterior, Rachel suspected Charlotte's intelligence would be a match for Marjorie's.

When they arrived in Creams, you wouldn't have known there'd been a storm the night before. Passengers were out and about, having got through the nightmare of the night before, with many heading to the Coral Restaurant for breakfast.

Rachel indicated to the server that they wanted a table for two.

"This way, Chief." The server led them to the rear, which brought back memories of where she had often met with her best friend Sarah and with Marjorie.

"What can I get you, Chief?" asked Charlotte, clearly aware there was a supplemental charge in Creams.

"Please call me Rachel," said Rachel. "And this one's on the house. Take your pick."

"In that case, I'll have a cream bun, please, Greg," she looked at the server, who grinned. "I haven't had breakfast yet. And a pot of coffee."

"So, your usual, ma'am?" Greg said.

Charlotte was obviously a regular at Creams.

"You got it."

"And for you, Chief?"

"Just coffee, please."

While Greg left to prepare their orders, Rachel studied Charlotte. As suspected, her mind was razor sharp, and she had a good head for names and faces, making Rachel feel that the story about meeting Eleanor before was true. "I heard the captain announce breakfast would be served until eleven o'clock this morning," said Rachel, making polite conversation while they awaited Greg's return. The cruise line would do everything it could to compensate passengers for the horrendous discomfort they'd experienced through the night, not to mention the countless injuries that Sarah and her team had no doubt treated.

Chapter 13

Once the coffees and Charlotte's cake were served, Rachel asked, "Perhaps you could tell me what you know about Eleanor Brodie?"

Charlotte's bright green eyes bored into Rachel's as she looked up at her. "Not a lot really," she said. "The last time we met, we were on a maiden voyage."

Rachel raised an eyebrow. "I see, and was that aboard one of our cruise ships?"

"Yes, the *Meridian Queen*. It was the *Meridian*'s maiden voyage – I said that already, didn't I? – beautiful ship with state-of-the-art technology. I had a wonderful time. We toured the Caribbean and then Hawaii before returning to Florida. This will be my first time in Greenland," she said, "and after last night, I might not repeat it in a hurry," she added with a chuckle.

Rachel couldn't help smiling. The ship was due to arrive in Nuuk, Greenland, the next morning before sailing on to other ports around the island. No further storms were forecast, and although it would be cold, that was only to be expected when visiting an Arctic island.

"It's my first visit too," said Rachel.

"Are you new to working on this ship?"

"Yes, although I've cruised on board many times."

"Is your husband with you?"

Rachel smiled again. Charlotte didn't miss a trick. "No. My husband is a private investigator in England.

This is a temporary assignment – six to nine months at the most."

"What made you want to leave home and work on a cruise ship?"

Rachel scratched her head. "There were a number of reasons, but mostly I needed a change from what I was doing and a new challenge."

"I can't imagine your husband is happy letting a woman as beautiful as you out of his sight," Charlotte said, wiping her mouth after finishing her cake.

Rachel chuckled. "Carlos is rather handsome himself; we trust each other."

"Carlos? Is he Spanish?"

"No, he's Italian, raised in England. His ancestry lies somewhere in Colombia, and his father wanted to honour the Spanish side, so he went against tradition and named him Carlos, rather than Carlo."

"And the Jacobi part of your surname, is that your husband's side?"

"Yep. He's got some Jewish heritage in there too." Rachel couldn't believe how much personal information Charlotte had extracted from her in such a short space of time.

"I take it you don't have children."

It was a statement rather than a question. "You take it, right," said Rachel, feeling more uncomfortable with that topic.

"Me neither. I'm glad, actually, because I married

a complete waste of space. He married me for my money and was a lazy toad who spent most of his time riding my horses instead of working. He claimed he couldn't get a job, but he was just a no-good waster. In the end, I got wise to him and decided looks weren't everything. He was handsome enough, but nowhere near interesting enough. In fact, he was the three D's."

"The three D's?" quizzed Rachel.

"Drab, dull, and dim."

Rachel laughed.

"Dull as ditchwater, I believe you English say."

Rachel laughed again as she took a sip of coffee. The laughter relieved her tension. If she wasn't trying to investigate a murder, she would enjoy spending a lot more time with Charlotte Kieft. But it was time to get to the point.

"Back to Eleanor Brodie. What makes you think I might have arrested her?" asked Rachel.

"Well, you're the chief of security, and a man who was watching her died on a previous sailing – his might not be the only death related to her – hell, for all I know, she could cruise the world, knocking passengers off left, right and centre. I read about people going overboard all the time."

"It's not as common as all that," said Rachel, taking on a reassuring tone.

"Has she killed somebody on this cruise?"

"No," said Rachel firmly. "But can you tell me anything more about her and the man who died?"

"We met when I sat next to her at a VIP dinner on the previous cruise."

Rachel's ears pricked up. "What sort of VIP dinner?"

"Similar to the one I'm attending tonight."

"With a celebrity chef hosting, you mean?"

"Exactly. In fact, it was Belinda Marlow who hosted that one too. She's brilliant, although pricey. Anyhow, that's where I met Eleanor. I assumed if I didn't catch up with her today, she'd be there tonight. She seemed to know the chef."

Now, Rachel was really listening; the chef, Belinda Marlow, was becoming more and more interesting, as was Charlotte Kieft. "And what do you know about her?"

"Not much. She was secretive, but as I said, there was a man watching her the whole time. I wondered if he was an ex stalking her."

"You're very observant," said Rachel.

"I watch a lot of murder detective programmes and true crime. When you get to my age and you're divorced with no children, other than the four dogs and Flame."

"Flame?"

"My mare. Unfortunately, I can't ride her too much anymore, and if I do, I have to go side saddle – the hips aren't what they used to be, although I'm fit enough. I have a ranch hand who rides her most days."

Rachel guessed Charlotte was in her late seventies, but she'd find out later as she needed to corroborate this story and look into what happened to the man on the *Meridian Queen*.

"Do you know the man's name?"

"No. But the man who had been watching her fell overboard; that's what they said anyways. I felt that was suspicious and told your lot on that cruise ship, but they weren't interested. They thought I was a dotty old woman jumping to conclusions."

Rachel frowned and sighed. Charlotte Kieft was anything but dotty.

"And is there anything else you can tell me?" said Rachel.

"Not really," said Charlotte, finishing her coffee. "What about you? Is this going to be a fifty-fifty sharing?"

Rachel smiled, and Charlotte shrugged.

"I thought not. Anyway, Chief, I've probably given you enough to think about. I hope you've arrested her if she killed that man. Oh, hang on a minute. From the questions you've been asking, you haven't, have you? Something's happened to her."

Rachel found this woman far more astute than she'd initially imagined. "I'm sorry, Charlotte. I can't say but thank you for your help. And I will look into the incident on the previous cruise. Trust me."

"Oh, I do," said Charlotte. "You have an honest face

and an open demeanour, far more so than your predecessor." So she knew Jack Waverley as well.

"I always travel with Queen Cruises," said Charlotte, by way of explanation. "Anyways, Chief, I expect you have more important things to do than entertain a dippy old woman."

Rachel would have loved to chat more, but there was too much going on, and she still needed to have a word with Clint Foster.

14

Rachel felt bad for not being honest with the team, unable to explain what only a few of them knew. She couldn't do that because she was under orders, but she also needed to know who she could trust. Sharing anything beyond the usual was going to be difficult. Her close circle included Jason, a close friend and her best friend's husband, as well as Rosemary Inglis and Ravanos, both of whom she had got to know before becoming chief of security. She knew each one well enough to trust them completely. Tamara Shutt had to be included because of her orders, but Rachel wasn't ready to let her in on everything. As for the rest of the security team, she was still getting to know them. Before the events of last night, a small number had already been giving her sleepless nights.

In the meeting, they discussed the crimes being

investigated since the ship had left Iceland and their ongoing monitoring of a minority who were causing headaches below deck.

Rachel delegated members of the team to look into these issues, particularly a spate of thefts from passenger staterooms by an opportunist wearing a navy-blue hoodie who kept their head hidden from security cameras. Stateroom attendants had been alerted to be on the lookout for the person, and to be diligent when working in passengers' rooms.

Overall, the meeting went well, and most were so tired in the storm's aftermath that they didn't ask too many questions. This was a good thing because it meant Rachel didn't have to lie. With the meeting concluded and various tasks delegated, the team dispersed to continue with their duties. Rachel looked at Clint Foster.

"I need to discuss something with you. Please wait outside while I speak to Jason and Rosemary," she said.

Clint's ruddy face turned an even deeper crimson, but he said nothing as he left with the others. She saw him grumbling to a couple of his fellow troublemakers before taking a seat outside her office. Tamara looked miffed at being left out of the inner circle but would continue with her assigned CCTV trawl.

"How's Sarah?" Rachel asked Jason.

"She's fine. Thankfully, it wasn't as serious as Doctor

Bentley thought, but she's not happy about being ordered to take today and tomorrow off."

Rachel smiled. "That's reassuring. If she's fighting, it means no real harm's been done."

"What did you find out from Alex Reyes?"

"It turns out Eleanor worked for MI6."

"British overseas intelligence?" Rosemary quizzed.

"Yes. She was looking into something I'm not at liberty to discuss and employed him without her bosses knowing. That helps us because it puts us in a position where whoever killed her knows nothing about him. He might be useful because he has inside knowledge and isn't unknown to the security services. But he's scared. I don't think he realised how dangerous her mission was going to be. He confirms she was meeting a mole on board the ship."

"I don't suppose he named this source?" Jason checked.

"No. To be honest, Eleanor didn't tell him much at all."

"Sounds like whoever it was turned out to be a double agent," said Rosemary.

"That's the working theory, unless the person was late and someone else got to her first," said Rachel, scratching her head. "What did you find out about the two crewmen caught on CCTV stumbling around?"

"Nothing suspicious," said Rosemary. "Both were where they should be and both arrived in the places they were meant to. I don't believe there's anything of interest there."

"Okay, so we'll rule them out for now. I went through Eleanor's stateroom and found a few things," said Rachel. "I also discovered something interesting. I don't know how relevant it is yet, but we need to take it seriously."

Jason's eyelids were red and swollen. She would try to keep this brief so he could take care of Sarah and hopefully get some rest. "While I was going through Eleanor's room, her neighbour knocked, saying she was concerned Eleanor hadn't returned to her room. She heard her leave around the time that would fit in with her going straight to the laundry. This woman, Charlotte Kieft, is Texan. I've carried out a brief background check and she is who she says she is, a wealthy American with a ranch in Texas."

Rosemary grinned.

"Some people have all the luck," said Jason.

"Charlotte spends half her life cruising and the rest on the ranch. Because she interrupted me, I'll ask Ravanos to go through Eleanor's room again."

"Did you find anything?" Rosemary asked.

"Just these." Rachel opened the safe and placed the evidence bag containing the items she'd picked up in Eleanor's room on her desk.

The others looked at the contents without touching the bag.

"Tomorrow, she's got a private tour followed by a dinner for two at the Hotel Hans Egede. I intend to attend both."

"Dinner with Alex, do you think?" Jason asked.

"I haven't had time to ask him, but I doubt it. She would avoid being seen with him in public. If you're okay with it, I'll take Sarah with me."

"It'll do her good... I think," Jason sounded hesitant.

"Don't worry, she'll be safe. Also, Eleanor has a ticket to the celebrity chef dinner tonight. It's worth looking into. I have to be there anyway, but I'd like Rosemary and Ravanos to be in the background."

"What about me?" Jason asked.

"Your duty lies with your wife, but you'll have plenty of work to do on your laptop. We need to know if Eleanor was meeting people at the dinner and if so, who. It would be useful to have Alex at the dinner tonight in case he recognises anyone. Could you arrange for him to have a ticket, Jason?"

"Consider it done, boss."

She smirked, still not used to him calling her boss. Having worked in the police, she was accustomed to this rank-and-file stuff, so she would get used to it.

"Her passport's in the bag, along with badges." Rachel tapped the evidence bag. "Pinned to three crew uniforms in her wardrobe."

Rosemary's eyes were like saucers. "Seriously... besides yours?"

"Yep. A junior IT officer's uniform, engineering overalls, and a member of the kitchen staff. Perhaps you could find out if the badge names are aliases once you've had some sleep, Rosemary?"

"I'm running on adrenaline right now. I'll do it as soon as we're finished here."

"Keep it between us three, and Ravanos, please. It would be useful to know what she was going to do in each of those areas, but we might never know. Still, start with the IT officer, and if she was using a real name, look at her access levels," she said. "That could be a lead."

"The most interesting finding came via Charlotte Kieft, Eleanor's seventy-eight-year-old neighbour, who reminds me of Marjorie Snellthorpe."

Jason grinned. "She must be interesting."

"Charlotte says she met Eleanor on another cruise nine months ago. It was the *Meridian Queen*'s maiden voyage, incorporating the Caribbean and Hawaii. Charlotte tried to speak to Eleanor when she recognised her, but Eleanor pretended not to know her."

"Do you think Charlotte made a mistake, or that Eleanor didn't want to draw attention to herself?" asked Jason.

"The latter is my assumption. She must have been horrified to be next door to a woman she'd met before."

"How can we be sure this lady isn't imagining things?" Rosemary asked.

"Charlotte says they met at a celebrity chef event on the *Meridian Queen*, hosted by the same celebrity chef..."

"Who was wandering around the crew-only area in the early hours," finished Rosemary.

"Was she now?" Jason said.

"Precisely," said Rachel. "I don't like coincidences. We need to look into this chef, which is why I want Alex to attend this evening in case he knows her. We have to be careful because Peter Jenson's attending, along with other senior officers like me and a room full of high-value cruisers. Whatever happens, we mustn't cause a stir."

"So who gave Belinda Marlow access to the crew-only area? Oh, don't tell me." Jason nodded towards the door where Clint Foster was waiting outside.

"I take it he didn't check with you either?"

"No."

"That man's a dinosaur," said Rosemary. "Sorry, I hate talking about a member of the team, Chief, but he really is."

Rachel was aware Clint could be misogynistic. He had tried to make her life difficult since her first day as chief of security. She'd made allowances and given him enough time to adapt, but his determination to undermine her may now put them in a dangerous situation. It was time to have a word, and if that didn't yield results, she would speak to Peter Jenson about getting him transferred at the earliest opportunity.

"There's no point in having dissent in the ranks, and if he will not toe the line, he needs to go," she said. "I don't have the time or the mental bandwidth to deal with him anymore. This is strictly between us." If he would not respect her leadership, neither would he respect the next person coming in when she finished her secondment, as that was also a woman. It was time to deal with Clint Foster.

Rachel pushed down the anger rising in her chest and wondered if she should have this conversation after she'd had some sleep. No. Best to get it out of the way.

"So that's it for now. When you've had a rest, Jason, I need you to look into the *Meridian Queen*'s maiden voyage. Charlotte Kieft says a man who had been watching Eleanor went overboard."

"You think Eleanor killed him?" said Jason.

"It's a possibility, isn't it? It might also be the ramblings of an older lady who likes to gossip. We have a duty to look into it. If the guy was a foreign agent or someone with nefarious intent, perhaps that time Eleanor came out on top."

"Unlike this time," said Rosemary. "We'll do anything we can to help."

Rachel sighed heavily. "Thank you. At the moment, it's a muddy pond. You put your hand in, stir it around, and more mud comes to the surface. But between the three of us, and Ravanos, we'll get to the bottom of it.

Were Graham, Gwen, and Bernard happy to keep the details of how Sarah was injured quiet?"

"Yes," said Jason. "The story is that Sarah fell and injured herself, which is the truth."

"Good. Is there anything else you need to tell me about the CCTV, Rosemary?"

From Rosemary's report, she and Tamara had spotted Eleanor twice, but Eleanor knew exactly where the ship's CCTV cameras were and avoided them.

"Nope, just those few times mentioned in my private report. Interesting that Charlotte Kieft heard her leave her stateroom because I checked the CCTV from the corridor once we knew her room number. But there was nothing from last night."

"So you think this video-blocking technology Tamara mentioned might be real?" said Rachel. She noticed Jason's confusion. "Rosemary can tell you about it."

"I've got video of her going into her room at about eight o'clock. I went right through to the early hours when she was killed. And as far as the technology is concerned, she didn't leave her room."

Rachel felt her lips thinning. This was a worry. "Alex doesn't think she would carry anything other than decoys, but if someone has stolen that sort of technology from her, how do we find them?" Her heart pounded.

Jason shook his head. "She had nothing on her, not even a phone. Was her phone in her room?"

"No," said Rachel. "We have to assume that whatever technology she had on her person – video blocking or otherwise – and her phone is with whoever killed her. We can only hope Alex is right that if she was carrying anything, it would be decoys. We have her smartwatch and a micro-SD card to investigate, but I don't want anyone outside this room knowing about them. I'm also assuming the killer took the cloned access card and although mine's reconfigured, we can check if the clone is used again. It might give us a lead."

"I'll make regular checks on that," said Rosemary.

Rachel nodded. "And keep trawling CCTV and see if Eleanor, or whoever she was meeting, slipped up at any time. It might help us find her source; otherwise, we need to flush them out," said Rachel.

"How?" asked Jason.

"I don't know, but we need to work on it. If her story turns out to be true, I wonder if Charlotte might be useful in an observation role."

"That's risky," said Jason.

"I realise that," replied Rachel. "But she's as sharp as a razor, and I think she'd be up to the task as long as we keep her safe." *Involving Charlotte in any way would be a desperate measure, though*, Rachel thought. Knowing that the entire fleet could be at risk of a cyber-attack might just call for a desperate measure. She also had to consider that, however unlikely, Charlotte herself might be a spy.

"Are you sure she'd be willing?" asked Rosemary.

Rachel grinned. "She'd already decided that Eleanor murdered the man on the previous cruise, so yes. I think she would. The question is, am I? My dilemma, as well as her safety, is what to tell her. If I tell her too little, she could put herself at risk, and if I tell her too much, I'll be going against all protocol."

It was Jason's turn to smirk. "That wouldn't be the first time."

"No," said Rachel, chuckling. "But before, I had nothing to lose; now, I've got a job."

"Who's worried about the job you didn't want in the first place?" he said.

"You make a good point, but I wouldn't have taken it if a certain person had accepted it like they should have," she replied with a grin.

Jason frowned. "I've never been a leader but I'm a good second-in-command."

"Better than good," said Rachel, locking away the evidence bag before her meeting with Clint Foster. "Okay, let's do what we have to do for now."

15

Clint Foster was built like a heavyweight boxer. His attitude problem was not dissimilar to that of many police officers Rachel had encountered, but they had mostly been someone else's problem. This man was her problem. His records revealed he was one of the longest-serving security officers on former Chief Waverley's team, which explained why Waverley had tolerated him for so long.

Rachel wasn't short at five feet ten, but Foster towered over her at six feet three inches and was three times as broad.

"Please take a seat, Clint. Would you like a tea or coffee?"

The chair opposite her desk groaned in protest as he sat down, his attitude barely disguised as polite.

"No, let's get on with this. What can I do for you?"

Okay, so he didn't want to make small talk, but this interview would be conducted at her pace and in her way, not his. "How are you?" she asked.

Confusion spread across his face. The question took him by surprise; she'd meant it to.

"I'm fine. Why do you ask?" He folded his arms in front of his chest, his body language defensive.

"I just wondered if you were coping with your workload, that's all."

His dark green eyes bulged as he shifted his hands to the arms of the chair. It groaned again as he gripped its arms. "What are you implying? I'm well able to do my job without any—" He cut himself off from whatever insult he would have added.

"And yet there have been issues..." Rachel let the words hang in the air. "I wondered if things were getting on top of you."

"I can do my job, much better than—"

Again, he cut himself off. He had been about to say, 'better than you.' If only he could understand what she'd dealt with during the night, but that would remain well away from his ears.

"You seem distracted," she said. "And I wondered if something was wrong."

He gripped the arms of the chair so tightly that Rachel wondered if they might crumble like they did in films. "Who said I'm distracted? What are you accusing me of?"

Rachel had expected a reaction to her challenge, but the strength of it surprised her. Now she wondered if he really had something going on in the background. She made a mental note to check if he had any health issues or financial worries. "It's just something that's been noticed. And I take an interest in every person in 'my' team." She emphasised 'my' to make it clear who was in charge.

"Yeah, well, your predecessor knew who he could trust to get on with things," Clint replied. "And I was his number one go-to guy."

Funny, he never mentioned that to me, thought Rachel. Waverley had given her a detailed handover and background on each person in the team she'd be leading. He'd suggested she might have trouble with a quartet of long-serving security officers who, as Waverley had put it, needed a kick up the backside. She wished he'd done the figurative kicking himself rather than leaving it to her. Men like Clint might have taken it better from him. Still, here she was, trying to sort out an issue she'd inherited.

"So is it safe to say that you are coping and managing with the day-to-day requirements of being a security officer?" she asked, not taking her eyes off his face. As it grew redder, it also became blotchy. Face stubble showed he'd been called to duty earlier than expected, as he usually shaved. His nose looked as though it had been broken in the past, and he had a scar above his left eyebrow. She could just about make out the tattoo of a woman's long mane protruding above the collar of his shirt. His heavy build was half fat, half muscle. Rachel concluded he probably spent more time in the gym than he did doing his job, and certainly not before his early shifts, or she'd have come across him when she went to work out after a run.

He leaned forward, his eyes challenging. "Nobody's ever questioned my ability to do this job. You realise I was a detective in the Los Angeles Police Department?"

He must think her an idiot if he imagined she hadn't read his file. He never got beyond Police Officer. Attitude had always been his problem, yet somehow, he kept this job, a job that she increasingly believed he should leave. His attitude towards senior officers and his prejudice against women were always going to be there. He'd been twice divorced, and domestic violence, although not proven, had been mentioned in the file. Looking at him glowering across the table at her, she could believe it. Maybe the force had turned a blind eye, or the woman had dropped charges. There were no recorded incidents since he joined the ship's security team, but as far as she could gather, he preferred drink to women these days. Waverley mentioned nothing like that, but he kept a tight rein on his staff and wouldn't have tolerated any violence from within his team, especially not violence against women. It was anathema to him.

Rachel chose not to challenge the lie about his previous status. "We've established that you believe you're coping with your job," she thought, despite having a female manager.

"Nobody's ever questioned it," he reiterated.

She picked up his file. "That's not entirely true, is it? There have been a few incidents where your ability to cope under stress has come into question."

He was shifting in his chair as if uncomfortable; the chair was threatening to buckle. Rachel regretted not having Jason with her, but she had felt that would be counterproductive, signalling to Clint that she couldn't manage him. She just hoped that having the desk between them would give her enough protection and time to press the emergency button should she need it. Failing that, her karate black belt training should prevent him from causing her too much damage should he lose it.

He let go of the chair, waving the air. "Misunderstandings. Nothing recent."

"One issue that has come to my attention is your timekeeping. You've arrived late for your shift on half a dozen occasions over the past month. It would be remiss of me not to monitor that. Now you've assured me you have nothing affecting your performance." She stared him down, and eventually, like all bullies, he dropped his eyes and looked away, but not for long.

He lifted his head, glaring at her. "You've only been on the ship for two minutes; you've no idea what these shifts are like. It's not always easy to climb out of bed when you've only just got in it."

She couldn't recall an occasion where he'd had to climb out of bed having just got to it, whereas she could list many occasions where that had happened to her over the three weeks since she'd taken over from Waverley.

"We can monitor it, and if needs be, and if you can't get to shift on time, we can always look at reducing your hours, which would obviously include a reduction in pay."

Now his fists clenched, signalling it was time to move the conversation on to what was more important to her. She'd made her point.

"What can you tell me about Belinda Marlow?"

His thick-set jaw and lips flipped from all-out aggression to derision as a smirk crossed his face. "So that's what's bothering you, is it? Trodden on your dainty toes, have I?"

Rachel held his gaze, although her heart was pounding in her chest. Not wanting this to escalate out of control, she said, "I'll repeat the question. What can you tell me about Belinda Marlow?"

"I gave her permission to access the kitchens. She's done it before when hosting events for Queen Cruises."

"As I understand it," said Rachel, picking up a folder and opening it at the right page, "any behind-the-scenes access for passengers and others not directly employed by Queen Cruises must be approved by the Chief of Security or their deputy if the chief is not available. Did you speak to my deputy?"

"Look, don't bellyache over it. She asked me if she could have access, and I didn't see a problem with it. I signed it off; it's no big deal."

Rachel sighed. "The deal is, Clint, that you didn't follow procedure. You haven't run it past me or Jason Goodridge. Neither of us would have known she had behind-the-scenes access if we hadn't picked it up on CCTV."

"What were you doing checking CCTV?"

She sighed again. "It's my job to know what goes on and who has access to where, as long as I'm Chief of Security on board this ship."

"Yeah, well, you probably need to back off a bit, otherwise your precious little toes might get sore from being trodden on."

"I suggest you be very careful before you say anything else, Foster," said Rachel, resorting to dropping his first name. She'd had enough.

"Okay, so now you know she has access. What do you want from me?"

"I will make a note of this in your file, and I would like reassurance that you will not go behind my back again. And let me warn you, if you do, I will raise it as a disciplinary strike."

"Fine," he muttered.

"And an apology." She knew she was pushing him, but it had to be done.

"What?"

"You need to apologise for going against procedure."

"You're kidding, right?"

"Do I look as if this is a joke?"

"Fine."

That was as much as she was going to get from him without making it a mountain. "And I'll ask one final time. Are you coping with your workload?"

He glared at her, muttering through gritted teeth. "Yes."

"Yes, what?" said Rachel.

He inhaled deeply, his whole body shaking with rage. It was going to stick in his throat, but she had to win this battle.

"Yes, Chief," he grunted.

"Thank you; you're dismissed," she said.

With an attitude that made Rachel wonder if Clint was about to throw the chair across the room, he stood, albeit stiffly, and swaggered from the room, attempting to hold his head high as if he hadn't just been given a lecture by the headteacher.

If it wasn't serious, it would be laughable. One thing was certain: Clint Foster was on her radar, and she was going to keep a very close eye on his behaviour and actions for as long as she remained in post. People like him were dangerous, and insubordination on a cruise ship like this could be lethal.

16

Rachel tapped lightly on Sarah's door, not wishing to disturb her if she was asleep.

"Coming," Sarah called, then opened the door.

Rachel entered the balcony stateroom, which was similar to her own. Officers were allocated staterooms on deck twelve, accessed via a staff-only door. She was delighted to see a lot more colour in her friend's cheeks than when she'd found her in Alex Reyes' room. Her hair was wrapped in a towel, and she wore her own dressing gown rather than the standard white one the ship provided. "It's good to see you looking more like yourself."

"Can you believe they won't let me work when we all need to pull our weight?"

"I think you've done enough for now, so enjoy it while you can," said Rachel, walking into the sitting room and flicking the switch on the kettle. "It's a good thing," she added, wondering why Jason wasn't with her.

"It's infuriating, that's what it is. I feel absolutely fine and hate leaving the team in the lurch. I feel like a complete failure for letting them down."

"What a pity everyone on this ship doesn't have your work ethic," said Rachel, still annoyed from her conversation with Clint.

"Uh-oh, are you having trouble?"

"What do you know about Clint Foster?"

Sarah rolled her eyes. "I wondered if you might have problems with him. He's a male chauvinist if ever I met one. Even Jason has trouble with him, and he's a man. You know how Jason gets along with most people."

"He never said anything until today, but I guess he didn't want to influence me. It's always best to let people come to their own conclusions, and I came to mine a while ago. I don't get his attitude. It's not as if I haven't met people like him before, but most of them at least try to conceal their resentment. I should have had Jason in the room with me before I spoke to him just now. That could have been a mistake, but I didn't want him to see me as weak."

"I think you need a strong coffee," said Sarah, taking over the kettle while Rachel flopped into a chair.

"His reactions were over the top. You don't know of any illness he might have, do you?"

"Not unless arrogance is an illness."

"He might have been less hostile with a witness in the room, but at least I've seen him at his worst and came out without being punched. That's a plus."

Sarah's eyes widened as she handed Rachel a strong mug of coffee. "That hostile, huh?"

Rachel picked up the mug, happy to let off steam. "Did you realise my precious little toes have been trodden on?"

Sarah burst out laughing. "Oh my word, he didn't say that, did he?"

"Yep," said Rachel. "Word for word. He's a throwback from America's Wild West. I don't know how anyone with that big an ego gets through life."

"Unfortunately, you get more of his type in security than in other jobs on board, and you've met your share in the police force. We had a few of them in my hospital days too, and not just patients."

"There are Clint Fosters in every walk of life," said Rachel, smiling before the list got any longer.

"At least you've cheered me up," Sarah sipped the tea she'd brewed for herself.

"I thought Jason told me he was looking after you?" Rachel said.

"Fussing like a mother hen, you mean. He had to pop out for some tech part he needed and wanted to call someone to stand in for him. I told him if he valued his marriage, he'd better not. He'll be back any minute.

Graham said I could leave the infirmary on the condition I have someone with me for twelve hours."

"Yeah, Jason told me. It makes sense. Now for the good news. As you've got a day off tomorrow, would you like to join me on an impromptu tour and have lunch in Greenland? Only if you're up to it."

"Really?" Sarah's green eyes lit up.

"It's work for me, I'm afraid, but we can make the most of it."

"Intriguing," said Sarah. "And yes."

"Eleanor Brodie booked a private tour and lunch for two. It might be nothing, but I thought I'd go in case it turns out to be important."

"Whatever the reason, I'll be glad to get out." Sarah finished her tea and removed the towel from her head, patting it dry.

"Hopefully no-one will recognise me as the chief of security. We both look different out of uniform and with our hair down."

"If you throw on some makeup as well, this dinner date might make a pass at you."

"Don't be ridiculous," said Rachel. "Are you sure you want to come? You can decide tomorrow if you like."

"I'm coming. And Greenland isn't often on our itinerary, so I'll be glad to."

"After last night's storm, I'm not surprised it's not a regular," said Rachel. "It wouldn't be on mine at all if I were planning the cruises."

"Storms are usually worse around Iceland, and Greenland is beautiful," said Sarah. "I have been there once before, but you can't get too much of a good thing. In all seriousness, I wouldn't want you going on your own anyway; it might be dangerous."

Rachel had considered that too and wondered if taking Sarah with her was wise. She would keep her friend safe at all costs. She finished her coffee. "It's most likely a dead end." She yawned. "I'm so tired."

"To be honest, so am I. In a way, it will be nice having the rest of the day off. I'll be able to sleep."

"I'm surprised they're letting you sleep. I mean, you had a head injury; aren't you supposed to stay awake?"

"It looked worse than it was. I'm fine. In fact, my shoulder's the sorest."

"Mine too," said Rachel, watching her friend tease the brush through her long brown hair.

"Tell me about Alex. What did you find out about him and Eleanor Brodie? Jason hasn't said much."

"Eleanor worked for British Intelligence and employed Alex in a private capacity. She wasn't the most trusting of people, but considering she's now dead, that's understandable. From what I can gather, she was looking into something that I can't talk about."

"And Alex was her backup? I'm not sure she made the right choice there; he's unpredictable."

"You're right. I think she hired him for tech support, and he's an unknown quantity. What Eleanor was looking into has something to do with the blackout, but I'm sure you gathered that."

"As we've had nothing like that before, yes."

Rachel smiled. "On a lighter note, I've met Marjorie the Second." Just thinking about Charlotte Kieft brought a smile to Rachel's face. She really hoped her judgement of the woman was sound.

"You've got to be kidding me! Who?"

"She's in the room next door to the former Eleanor Brodie." Rachel got up and made them both another hot drink.

"Anyway, this passenger met Eleanor on a previous cruise, where she says a man went overboard."

"Blimey," said Sarah, taking the tea from Rachel and putting her brush on the table.

"She's as bright as Marjorie. Maybe ten years younger, and talks for England, or should I say Texas? Because she's from Texas."

"She sounds amazing," said Sarah, chuckling.

"Anyway, this Charlotte Kieft is a mine of information. I'm just hoping the information she's given me is going to help."

"At least you've got a lead. And at least you know who the dead woman was now. That's something, isn't it?"

"Yep. We took fingerprints, which came back negative, but now I know she worked for MI6, I understand why. We're putting the pieces together, but there are still a lot of gaps. It's a mess. I almost wish Waverley was here."

"He'd have hated a blackout in the middle of the storm; injured passengers and a dead spy," said Sarah.

"That's what Peter said."

"Waverley's better off tending his garden with Brenda."

"I wish he'd dealt with Clint Foster before he left."

"I'm not sure anyone could do much about him without firing him."

"Well, that is an option I'm considering," said Rachel. "We sack people for less, I hear." Cruise lines could get rid of people a lot easier than public services in the UK.

"Do it then," said Sarah.

"It has to be a last resort. I've warned him; let that be enough for now. I don't want to be in the job for two minutes – as he put it – and become known as the person who fires people."

"Apart from a few, you wouldn't be disliked for getting rid of the likes of Clint Foster. Moving back to your investigation, apart from our outing tomorrow, do you have any other leads?" asked Sarah.

"A few," said Rachel. "Charlotte Kieft has given us something to look into."

"Is that surname Dutch?"

"You're good with names, aren't you? As is Charlotte;

she wheedled Carlos's name history out of me in five minutes over coffee in Creams."

Sarah grinned. "You must like her if you took her to Creams."

"It was her suggestion, which shows she has good taste," said Rachel.

"What else did she tell you?"

"That she met Eleanor at a celebrity chef dinner hosted by Belinda Marlow."

"Belinda Marlow, who's on this cruise?"

"The same," said Rachel.

"We're lucky to have her."

"Maybe, but that leads me back to the Clint problem. He gave Belinda Marlow unsupervised behind-the-scenes access. Not to mention without permission."

"Oh my. And Belinda's access is a problem, why?"

"I don't like that I wasn't informed about it, but that could just be my precious little toes being trodden on," Rachel said with a sardonic laugh. "But in a situation like this, where we have people going behind the scenes dressed as officers and a dead woman on our hands, I'd like to restrict access. It might well be nothing," she continued, "but I hate coincidences, and the fact that Belinda and Eleanor were both on a previous cruise bothers me."

"Lots of people who cruise regularly meet time and time again, Rachel. It might be nothing."

"We'll see, but for now I'm tired. I think I'm going to go to my office, and if I fall asleep, I fall asleep."

"That's a good idea," said Sarah. "Can't you go back to your room and take a nap?"

Saving Rachel the need to answer, Jason entered the room.

"As your husband is now here to make sure you don't go into some sort of head injury coma, I'll leave you to it."

Jason beamed at Sarah, crossing the room to kiss her on the head. "How are you feeling, darling?"

"I'll feel a lot better when people stop fussing over me, and I can go back to work."

"She's almost back to normal," said Rachel, laughing.

"Rachel invited me out on a tour in Greenland tomorrow. So at least I can occupy a day of my enforced leave."

"I'm pleased to hear it," said Jason. "It'll be good for you."

"How did your chat with Clint go?" Jason asked Rachel.

"As expected. But I think he got the message."

"So has Rachel," said Sarah, laughing. "Did you know she's got precious little toes to be trodden on?"

Jason raised an eyebrow.

Rachel gave a half smile, half grimace.

"He's got a nerve," Jason said, frowning. "Can I have a quick word outside, boss?"

"Oh, I love all this secrecy," said Sarah. "As if I can't keep a secret."

"This isn't about secrecy," said Jason. "It's doctor's orders."

"Fair point. Go on then, off you go. But remember, I'm supposed to be supervised, so don't keep him too long."

17

As they stepped out of Jason and Sarah's room, Rachel could see that Jason's face was serious. The lines under his eyes revealed how tired he was, and the lights accentuated the deep lines of concern.

"What is it?" she asked. The muffled sounds of officers enjoying their downtime created an unsettling contrast to the gravity she and Jason shared.

"I looked into the maiden voyage of the *Meridian Queen*, like you asked." Jason glanced both ways down the corridor before continuing. "Charlotte is right; a male passenger was reported missing halfway through the cruise, and he matches the description she gave you."

Rachel's stomach tightened. What had started as a strange coincidence might morph into something more sinister.

"Did they find him?"

"No, he's still missing, presumed dead," Jason replied, "but there's more to it. The stateroom attendant and a kitchen porter raised the alarm after he'd requested breakfast in his room but was nowhere to be seen. They discovered an empty whisky bottle and a spilled drink on the balcony. They were worried, so the housekeeping manager called security."

Rachel rubbed her head, carefully avoiding the dressing covering her injury. The wound throbbed constantly, a reminder of the horrendous night.

"It sounds as though he got very drunk and fell overboard," she said, but even as the words left her mouth, she didn't believe them.

"That was the conclusion," Jason confirmed with a sceptical lift of his eyebrow, "but there wasn't any footage of him falling. As you know, cameras monitor the edges of the ship for situations like that. Guess what? There was a CCTV glitch, which they put down to teething problems."

"This is sounding familiar." Rachel leaned against the wall, thinking about it. Most modern cruise liners had extensive camera coverage specifically designed to prevent – or at least document – anyone going overboard. A glitch similar to that on the M1 during the night was too convenient.

"Did they document Charlotte's concerns that he

might have been pushed?" she asked, already suspecting the answer.

"Nope. There was no mention of it anywhere." Jason crossed his arms, his posture rigid with frustration. "I've requested the full report, but the ship's crew followed procedure and reported it to the coastguard. The ship circled for a little while once they were made aware a passenger was missing, but as they were unable to determine where he went overboard, it was fruitless. The man's body was never recovered, but they were a male passenger short on disembarkation."

The corridor was now quiet apart from the gentle humming of the engines, in sharp contrast to the noises in her brain. Rachel tucked a strand of hair behind her ear while she processed.

"What was his name?" She had initially hoped she could dismiss Charlotte's report as coincidence, but now felt nauseous as the realisation dawned. Eleanor Brodie could have had something to do with the man's disappearance. Or worse – been responsible for it.

"Sam Akbar," Jason said. "His passport was American." He hesitated, shifting his weight from one foot to the other as he checked the corridor once more. "There's another interesting thing you will not like."

Rachel's nausea switched to a dull headache building behind her eyes.

"I think I can guess, but tell me anyway," she said, massaging her left temple.

"The man's a ghost," Jason whispered, leaning closer as an environmental officer passed by, giving them both a nod before going on shift. Jason waited until he was out of earshot. "Apart from boarding the *Meridian Queen*, he doesn't exist. When the ship returned to New York, they sent his toothbrush and hairbrush to the NYPD, but no DNA matches were found, and the man behind the passport, which was never found, didn't exist. If he was a criminal, he'd never been caught."

"Or his crime was wiped from the criminal database," said Rachel, feeling suddenly chilly.

"Exactly." Jason's eyes met hers. "We might be looking at another spy."

Rachel thought of Eleanor Brodie's body, cold and lifeless, in the ship's morgue. Two dead spies. Was one killed by the other on a previous sailing?

"Any family or next of kin?"

"Fictional. He had no home; an elderly couple had lived at the address he gave for over thirty years, and his background was fake. The passport registered with the cruise line had him down as American, but his whole life was false." Jason shrugged. "He could have been in witness protection, but I'm not sure how much time or how many brick walls the investigators hit. The cruise line didn't look into it once it was handed over, and the police dropped the case."

The hum of the ship's engines vibrated through the

soles of Rachel's feet. The *Coral Queen* continued its journey towards Greenland.

"So he could have been an American spy," she said.

"That's the question," said Jason with a grim nod. "We may never know."

"And Eleanor's not here to tell us," Rachel said, a heaviness settling in her chest while her headache worsened.

"Your only witness is Charlotte Kieft."

Rachel still considered Charlotte an innocent bystander who might know far more than she realised.

"Was there any other CCTV footage from the night he went missing?" Rachel asked, knowing surveillance was often their best ally – when there weren't irregular glitches, that was.

"Everything was given to the police," Jason replied.

"I wonder if we can access it?" Rachel mused, more to herself than to Jason. She glanced around, half expecting to see someone watching them.

"My guess is," said Jason, "if this is what we think, and the guy was a spy, there'll be a missing file and no CCTV."

Rachel felt frustration rising in her chest. Her hands clenched involuntarily at her sides. After years of solid police work, of following evidence and procedure, she was facing an adversary that played by different rules.

"This sort of thing scares me," she admitted, the confession tasting bitter. "You know, in the force, you deal with the dregs of humanity, but this spy stuff – it's out of my league."

She thought of her former cases in Leicester, and on this very cruise ship. How straightforward they seemed in comparison. They had patterns, rules, even. This was shadows within shadows, and she didn't like it.

"Obviously that kind of thing went on in the background when I was in the army, but it didn't filter down to us," Jason said, his eyes distant. "We just got orders based on intelligence and followed them to the letter. It didn't matter where the intelligence came from; we were just the guys shooting at each other without question." He leaned against the opposite side of his door, his broad shoulders slumping. "Not everything we did made sense, but we did what someone higher up thought was in the interests of national security. It's only when I think back that I ask questions, but then it ends up going down labyrinths I'd rather not follow."

Rachel could see the conflict in Jason's eyes – the soldier's discipline warring with the human being's need for answers. She understood it.

"And in the meantime," said Rachel, "lives are on the line, and people die."

"Yes," said Jason, his face souring. "All for the greater good or in the national interest."

"Okay, so it's probably not worth it, but please follow the case up as far as you can while you're with Sarah. Let me know if anything comes of it?" They needed to keep moving forward, even if it felt like swimming against a powerful tide.

"Do you want me to ask Tamara if she can find out anything? She's the whizz IT expert."

Rachel hesitated; she was under captain's orders to involve Tamara, but she still had her doubts. "Not yet," said Rachel. "I'd love to trust her, but..."

"You think she might work for the intelligence services?" asked Jason.

"I don't know." She couldn't tell him, was the reality that gnawed at her. "It's all this spy stuff. How do you trust these people? At the end of the day, their feet are in a different camp to ours – we just want to solve crime." Rachel wished she could tell Jason what Peter Jenson had said. And she might have to... later.

"You think she's a plant?"

Rachel sighed, exhaustion settling into her bones. Her head throbbed, both from the injury and the headache. "I need to get some rest, and you'd better get back to Sarah."

Jason put a hand on her non-sore shoulder and squeezed it gently. "You've got this, Rachel. We've got this. We'll find out who killed Eleanor Brodie, and if the powers that be want to brush it under the carpet after we do, that's up to them. But we'll do what we have to do."

The ship pitched slightly, a reminder of where they were and what they had been through.

"Our concern is keeping this ship and its passengers secure," said Rachel. To say nothing of the entire fleet went unsaid.

Jason gave her a quizzical look.

She shook her head apologetically. "Ignore me, I'm tired." The excuse was flimsy, but she couldn't share any more.

"I get you have to do what's necessary, Rachel, but if you need to talk, you can trust me."

"Thanks, Jason," replied Rachel, quickly cutting off the conversation before continuing solemnly. "It's not about trust; it's about orders."

"Right," Jason said, shrugging, before casually adding, "orders I understand."

Of course he did. His military background had trained him well.

"We'll speak later. You really had better check on your wife before she goes ga ga in there. Look after her." Rachel was still concerned about what might have happened to Sarah if Alex Reyes had turned out to be someone else.

"Sure will, boss." Jason grinned. "But she won't like it. She's an exceptional nurse, but she's a lousy patient."

As Jason disappeared back into his cabin, Rachel stood alone in the corridor. Eleanor Brodie, Sam Akbar, Charlotte Kieft – pieces of a puzzle she had to solve. Time to move. She turned and headed back downstairs to her office.

18

One floor of the Coral Restaurant had been commandeered for Belinda Marlow's VIP dinner. The original plan to erect a huge marquee on the lawn deck had been scrapped by the health and safety chief following the storm. The weather had improved dramatically throughout the day, but powerful gusts were still forecast. With three hundred ticket-holding passengers, those who dined informally would be accommodated in the set meal dining tier.

Peter Jenson and many of the senior officers were attending the celebrity-hosted dinner and were seated at tables with multiple time cruisers. Rachel would rather not attend in her formal capacity, but she hadn't been given a choice. She requested a table not too far from the one where Alex was sitting, looking uncomfortable.

Rachel had arrived early, scanning the area and studying the seating plan. She had a copy on her phone if needed. An excited buzz spread through the restaurant as guests arrived to take their seats. Initially, Rachel circulated, chatting to guests and pretending to enjoy the atmosphere while making mental notes about where everybody was. None deviated from the seating plan.

Belinda Marlow was in Rachel's sights. The forty-two-year-old had her brunette hair tied back in a sleek chignon for the evening. She wore a white silk above-knee dress that accentuated her curves. Belinda exuded confidence and comfort when speaking to the rich and powerful as she circulated. This was the first of her three ticketed charity events. While people took their seats, she made a point of speaking to a few from every table. Her smile and polite laughter came across as genuine.

Rachel had done her homework; the chef was immensely popular with passengers and crew for both her culinary creations and her charitable works. Rachel had visited the kitchens before arriving at the dinner and spoke to a couple of chefs. Even they, who could be fiercely territorial, spoke highly of her. Rachel made subtle enquiries about her behind-the-scenes access and was told Belinda made every effort to work with the teams of cooks to create her dishes. She was always hands-on when preparing a five-course gastronomic

Chapter 18

experience like that planned for tonight and had a PA who arranged everything beforehand so that things ran smoothly. Following these conversations, Rachel felt more relaxed about the chef's access, although she would still have preferred to know about it in advance.

As Rachel moved around the room, she observed wealth and extravagance in all its forms. With the tickets being highly priced, most attendees oozed affluence. Women's necks, wrists, and ears were adorned with diamonds, as if in competition to see who could carry the weightiest gems. Others wore more colourful jewels, like rubies, topaz, and sapphires – in fact, just about every gemstone known to the world. Designer watches were also on display; the trappings of riches adorned every neck, wrist, and finger. Only about a dozen seemed less ostentatious.

As the dinner was a formal event, the women wore elegant evening or cocktail dresses, and the men wore tuxedos with bow ties. Just a few wore black ties. Thankfully, Rachel only had to change into her formal officer's uniform for the evening. These uniforms were reserved for captain's dinners and special occasions such as this one. Hers included a white starched skirt and jacket, and she had chosen low-heeled shoes for the occasion. Rachel was more comfortable in jeans and t-shirts but had worn uniforms and then smart clothes throughout her career.

While staff circulated carrying trays of champagne

and non-alcoholic alternatives, Rachel mused on how many of the outfits for the evening would amount to months of wages for some of the crew.

Formal events were an interesting part of cruise ship life. On prior cruises, Rachel had attended VIP events with her dear friend Lady Marjorie Snellthorpe, but much of the wealth in this room was on a different level; several people were billionaires. Was the evening about raising money for charity, or were these people in danger?

A sudden tightness in her chest made her feel lightheaded.

"Get a grip, Prince," she told herself. "You should have tried for more sleep." She had tossed and turned for two hours this afternoon, trying to rest, but the pressing problems of a killer on the loose and a possible cyber-attack on the ship weighed heavily on her mind. She had given up and gone back to checking and double-checking everything she knew.

"Was Eleanor Brodie a member of British intelligence, as Alex Reyes claimed? If so, was she on the good or the bad side? And what was her link to the American Sam Akbar?" Rachel's mission to find a killer under such circumstances seemed impossible.

The weight of responsibility sat heavily on her shoulders this evening; she felt responsible not only for the safety of everyone in this room but also for thousands of other passengers. It didn't matter whether they had saved up all their lives for this cruise or whether the expenditure was like small change to them. Neither did it matter whether they were members of engineering struggling to send money back home to whatever country they came from.

Every life was precious to her. It wasn't just her job that made her feel that way; it was her ethos in life. Her father, being a vicar, had been her biggest influence growing up. Her faith gave her hope and the belief that every life was precious. She would do everything in her power to protect the lives of people on this ship.

She didn't have the big picture yet, but if protecting lives on the *Coral Queen* meant protecting lives on other ships, that's what she'd do.

Rachel heard a familiar voice to her left. Charlotte Kieft joined a table with five others. Rachel smiled at her. "Good evening, Charlotte."

"Good evening, Chief," the older woman replied. "I'm looking forward to this. The food at the last one was superb."

"Enjoy your evening," Rachel said before realising that almost every table was now occupied. She hurried to join her own table, smiling politely at the man on her right and the woman on her left.

19

"What's it like being the chief of security on a cruise ship?" the woman to Rachel's left, who had introduced herself as Maggie, asked.

"I can't reveal all the secrets, of course, but it's like being a detective in a floating city. Every day, there's something new and unexpected. At the same time, it's quite peaceful most days. Our main concern is ensuring that everyone on board stays safe and has a pleasurable journey." Rachel paused, her eyes crinkling with a hint of mischief. "And, of course, dealing with the occasional fight over sun beds or calming people who have imbibed a little too much alcohol when they get out of hand."

"I bet you have some stories to tell," said Maggie, chuckling.

If only you knew. Rachel smiled, her lips sealed. "Sometimes. But, as they say, what happens at sea stays at sea. Enough about me. How about you, Maggie? What brings you on this cruise?"

Maggie explained that she and her husband had always wanted to visit Greenland, but he passed away before they got the opportunity. She was travelling with their daughter to fulfil the dream.

"I'm from Washington DC," the man on her right, named Charles, said. "It sounds as if you have a lot more to do on board these vessels than I imagined?"

"Not compared to living in a city, and nothing you need to worry about," said Rachel.

She was happy to see the pre-appetisers arriving and people's conversations veering more towards the delicacies in front of them.

Rachel eyed Belinda Marlow's picture on the set menu, which was perched in the centre of the table. Her background revealed that she had been brought up in Dublin before moving to London, and then to Paris to train at a famous Michelin-starred hotel. She was responsible for earning another restaurant two Michelin stars but left three years ago to set up her own restaurant chain. Belinda's initial celebrity status came mainly from YouTube, where she had seventy thousand followers and regularly released videos showcasing her cooking techniques while keeping most of her recipes secret. Over the past twelve months, she had pivoted to TikTok, gaining an enormous following and creating many viral videos, posting two or three times a day. Rachel wondered how she found the time, but watching her this evening, she realised the woman was ultra-efficient and capable of leading.

With the amuse-bouche finished, the appetisers offered a choice between seared scallops with a champagne beurre blanc, served on a bed of micro greens, or sweetcorn velouté with truffle oil, and crispy pancetta. Rachel had opted for the scallops. The menu included gluten-free options for those with gluten sensitivity, and the servers already had a list of people with allergies, with allergen-free alternatives available. Belinda, or perhaps her PA, whom Rachel noticed hovering in the background, dishing out orders to staff, had thought of everything.

Rachel studied Charlotte, who appeared to be able to speak to anyone, as she was in deep conversation with the couple at her table. Rachel had decided against asking Charlotte to gather information; she couldn't justify putting the older woman's life at risk, no matter how urgent the situation was. She also had to consider that what might appear to be a coincidence – her being in a stateroom next door to Eleanor Brodie – might be exactly the opposite.

Alex continued to look uncomfortable at his table, constantly adjusting his bow tie as if it might strangle him. It might not have been a good idea to put him under this kind of pressure. He had already shown his terror when Sarah entered his room, but she had no choice: he was the only one who had had any contact with Eleanor, other than Charlotte.

Rachel tried to get his attention to send him a reassuring nod, but he was shifting nervously in his seat, picking at his food. She had put him in a situation he wasn't coping with. He was already sweating. She just hoped he would see something, anything, that would help them advance this investigation. Chasing criminals was always challenging, but pursuing invisible criminals who didn't show up on CCTV was something else. Rachel consoled herself with the fact that there was a time, as Marjorie often reminded her, when CCTV wasn't a luxury law enforcement officers had. Maybe she just had to rely on the basic skills of observation.

She wished Jason were here, but he had the evening off to stay with Sarah. While Sarah's twelve-hour official observation was over, Rachel wanted her to rest, and Jason needed to be sharp. He wouldn't be at his best unless he was sure his wife was well.

Tomorrow's another day, Rachel thought as she skipped the soup course. While the others at her table indulged, she glanced across the restaurant to see Rosemary walking slowly around. Rosemary's task was to seek out any of the few people Eleanor had been seen interacting with since boarding in Iceland. Rachel's attention would remain on the chef and Alex while pretending to be interested in the conversations taking place at her table. On other occasions, she would have enjoyed getting to know them, but her mind was too occupied.

The main courses elicited gasps of excitement and lots of exuberant praise from everyone around Rachel's table. About half, including herself, had opted for pan-seared halibut with saffron risotto and lemon caper sauce, while the rest chose Belinda's signature venison loin with juniper berry glaze, parsnip purée, and red wine-poached pear. Rachel couldn't fault what she had eaten so far, but she would decline dessert.

Captain Peter Jenson was doing an excellent job of appearing as though he didn't have a care in the world while chatting with those around his table. He was the ultimate professional, and Rachel admired him more the better she got to know him. Not all the department heads were at the dinner; Bert Holland and Aryna Petrova were absent, but their deputies were present.

With dessert over, it was time for the speeches. Belinda stood in front of the microphone, looking and sounding as though she was making an Oscar-winning speech.

"Good evening, ladies and gentlemen. I'm so pleased you could make it to our first dinner. Thank you for joining us tonight. I'm glad no-one has keeled over yet –

at least not from the food..." A ripple of laughter spread through the room. "The signature dishes you've indulged in tonight, I can assure you, nobody else has ever tasted before. They are brand new, which is why you've paid such a large sum of money to savour them."

Another ripple of laughter.

"As you know, the proceeds from this evening will be donated to maritime and homeless charities. While the tables are cleared, we'll move on to the next part of the evening before you are invited to the ballroom for a cocktail evening and dance. I'm offering a chance for three lucky people to join me in the kitchen after the ship sets sail again tomorrow afternoon. Our very own Captain Jenson has given me permission to auction this unique opportunity. You will learn how to set off smoke alarms, convince your loved ones that 'burnt' is a flavour, and perfect the art of ordering takeaways as a backup plan. So, roll up your sleeves, unbutton those wallets, and let the auction begin. Remember, a good cook always blames the ingredients!"

A third ripple of laughter rolled across the room. Rachel noticed a few people rolling their eyes. Wealthy individuals were used to being solicited for money for charity, and most of them didn't mind, but there were some who resented it, and were only here for the food and the celebrity status. Perhaps a few were here to network with their business colleagues.

Belinda moved away from the microphone to

rapturous applause as servers got on with their job of clearing tables and serving more wine. Rachel nodded to various members of staff and a few officers, excusing herself from the table and getting on her radio. Her first contact was Tamara.

"Anything to report?"

"Nothing, boss," came the reply. "CCTV's working everywhere without glitches."

Rachel moved into an empty serving bay where servers brought and distributed dishes during dinner. "That's great. Thanks. Any further sightings of our victim?"

"I've got her boarding, but she doesn't speak to anybody."

"Okay," Rachel said, "let me know if you notice anything strange, anything at all."

"I've got it, Chief," Tamara replied.

Rachel had no choice but to follow Peter Jenson's instructions and at least let Tamara do what she was good at, and what she was good at was detecting anomalies in security systems.

She radioed the chief of engineering. "How are things?"

Aryna sounded as gruff as she had that morning in Peter Jenson's quarters. "Everything's fine. We've got nothing to worry about."

"Let's hope not," she said, dialling her radio again to speak to Bert Holland.

"It's Rachel here. How are things your end?"

"All good. Nothing strange, no further anomalies since whatever happened in the middle of the night. It could just have been a storm, you know."

"Yeah," said Rachel, "let me know if you notice anything out of the ordinary."

"Of course," he snapped. Their reactions suggested both chiefs were on edge, but then she felt on edge herself. She had half expected something to happen during dinner, but all was normal so far. Belinda had behaved as one would expect a dinner host to behave, and Rachel hadn't spotted her spending more time with any one guest than with others.

Rachel had ensured Eleanor's ticket had been sold and placed a passenger of similar build and hair colour in the seat reserved for her. The passenger was unaware of the change because Rachel had rearranged place names before people entered for dinner. Ravanos was watching the passenger to make sure nothing happened to her. With dinner over and people circulating before the auction was about to begin, Rachel watched a man in a white tuxedo tap the passenger on the shoulder. When she looked around, he seemed surprised. A brief conversation followed, and then he returned to his seat.

Rachel's eyes were now glued to him as Belinda whispered in his ear, prompting him to get up and move to the side of the stage, mopping his brow with a handkerchief. Belinda took to the stage again.

"Ladies and gentlemen, please take your seats. It's now time for our auction. I've roped in one of your fellow guests to play auctioneer tonight. Please welcome Sam to the stage." The swarthy man with dark skin and jet-black hair that Rachel had been watching climbed onto the stage, taking the microphone to loud applause.

A clattering sound to Rachel's left drew her attention. Only a couple of people heard it.

Charlotte Kieft's champagne glass was on the floor, and her face had turned pale. The person in the seat next to her checked if she was okay, and a server cleared up the mess without fuss. Charlotte waved her neighbour's attention away reassuringly. Rachel didn't know whether to hurry across or stay and watch the man named Sam. Since he was occupied with auctioning the exclusive cookery lessons and she had his first name, it made more sense to check on Charlotte. She sidled over to Rosemary. "Monitor that man and find out who he is. There's something wrong with Charlotte; she knew our victim. I might be a while."

"No problem," said Rosemary, looking fresh from having had the afternoon to catch up on sleep. "Alex is keen to leave; he says he has seen nothing and doesn't know anyone."

"Let him go. It was a long shot anyway; Eleanor kept him in the dark."

Rachel watched Rosemary give Alex the nod. He left

while she subtly approached Charlotte's table, leaning down and whispering in her ear, "Are you all right?"

Charlotte's eyes appeared confused, and her complexion lacked colour. If it wasn't for her makeup, Rachel was convinced she'd be completely white.

"It's just – it's just…"

"Would you like to leave?"

"Actually, yes," replied Charlotte. "I have no need for cookery lessons on this scale, anyway."

"Take my arm," said Rachel gently. A few people at Charlotte's table shot her approving looks. Their focus shifted back to the auction once Charlotte was securely holding Rachel's arm. "Come on, let's get you out of here," said Rachel. She firmly yet kindly guided Charlotte, feeling the older woman trembling beneath her grip. Rachel supported her with each step forward. Both women moved from the room, where loud laughter and chatter continued. Sam was doing an excellent job of persuading people to raise their bids like an experienced salesperson. Rachel didn't believe for one moment he had been randomly selected for the role.

"Thank you, Rachel," Charlotte said. Once they were in the main corridors, Charlotte seemed to steady herself.

"Do you need to see a medic?" Rachel asked.

"No. I…"

"What is it?"

"That man..."

"Which man?"

"The man conducting the auction... He's... he's d-d-d-dead. At least he's supposed to be. That's the man who went overboard on the *Meridian*."

20

What a confusing turn of events, thought Rachel.

"Why don't I escort you back to your stateroom?" she said.

"I'd much rather have a nightcap, if that's all right with you."

"Certainly. Come with me," said Rachel, letting Charlotte walk by herself now that she was able. Rachel escorted her to the lifts and pressed the button for deck three.

"Where are we going?" asked Charlotte.

"I think it might be better if you come to my office so we can have a chat in private."

"If you say so, I'll be glad to sit down again. My legs feel incredibly weak," said Charlotte.

"It's adrenaline from the shock," said Rachel.

"I hope I'm not making a fuss over nothing."

"I'm sure you're not," Rachel said, swiping her pass at the locked office door. Charlotte wobbled again, so Rachel helped her onto the sofa in front of the coffee table.

"You wait there while I get us some drinks. What would you like?"

"A brandy, please."

Marjorie's favourite nightcap, thought Rachel, as she headed upstairs to the nearest bar. She ordered a brandy for Charlotte and a bottle of sparkling mineral water for herself.

When she got back, she placed her drink on the table, handing Charlotte the brandy. "There you are. That should help."

"Thank you so much. You've got a good heart, Rachel. I'm so sorry for the fuss, but I felt like I'd seen a ghost. I must have been mistaken about that man going overboard on the last cruise." Charlotte's eyes were full of confusion as she took a sip of brandy. "I could have sworn they said he had. And I'd seen him hanging about that woman, Eleanor... But maybe I was mistaken all along." Charlotte's words tumbled out of her mouth in her confusion.

Rachel didn't want to alarm her by telling her she was absolutely right and that a man had gone overboard.

"Are you certain it's the same man you saw on the *Meridian Queen*?" she asked.

"Oh yes, I never forget a face," said Charlotte. "It's one of my gifts. I'm almost photographic where names and faces are concerned. It's why I remembered Eleanor, even though she's changed her hairstyle and everything."

"Hm," said Rachel. "Tell me about this man."

"All I know is what I told you this morning. I saw him watching Eleanor all the time. At least that's what I thought at the time. He was always around her, and yet pretending not to be. I was worried for her, but I must have been wrong."

"About him watching her?"

"Possibly. I thought she'd murdered him or something. But it seems she hasn't. There I am, accusing her of an outrageous crime, and he's here, right as rain. I didn't see him around her this time, though."

Rachel looked at Charlotte, while pouring her water into a glass. "Did you see anyone else around her on this cruise?"

"There was a man at the dinner tonight, but she seemed to be avoiding him."

"Where was this?"

"By the pool. You know, the bit that's not monitored."

I might have guessed, thought Rachel. She took out her laptop and scrolled to the right image. "Was it this man?"

"Yes, that's him. I noticed him because it was a

similar situation to the one on the previous cruise with the man I thought had died."

Rachel raised an eyebrow. "In what way?"

"It was like they knew each other but pretended not to. She stopped when she saw him and turned around to go in the other direction."

At least it confirmed to Rachel what Alex had told her: that he was working with Eleanor, and probably under duress.

"Okay. And the man you saw tonight?"

"I'm sure he's the same man from the other cruise. Hang on a minute." Charlotte rifled through her handbag, pulling out her mobile phone and putting on her reading glasses. "I'll just switch this on. It's got all my photos. I'm sure I had one of him in the background because I showed it to the security officer on the *Meridian* when he interviewed me. It's odd, though, that they seemed to investigate, or half investigate, the disappearance. They asked me questions after I found out he was missing because I'd reported his strange behaviour to reception."

Once Charlotte's phone came to life, Rachel drank water while her new friend took an age to scroll through her photos.

"I really need to get somebody to put these into folders for me. My nephew's forever telling me I should. He's good at tech, you see. I'm not bad. I can take a photo and can find things... eventually anyways. And I can use all these latest messenger-type things to keep in touch with my nephew. I'm even on Facebook, but when it comes to things like storing and folders, I'm at a loss."

Rachel tried to remain patient, wondering if Charlotte might just be an attention seeker. But she'd been right about the man overboard situation, so if she was right about this, Rachel's headache was going to be coming back.

"Just a moment." Charlotte raised the glass to her lips, taking a large gulp of the brandy. "That feels better. Dinner was delightful, wasn't it?"

"Er, yes, it was," said Rachel. "Have you found what you're looking for?" she asked, keen to stick to the photo retrieval exercise.

Charlotte returned to squinting at her phone. "Ah, here it is." She handed her phone to Rachel, who used her fingers to enlarge the picture.

The photo showed an ice sculpture scene on board the ship, but there he was in the background – the man that Charlotte and the crew on board the *Meridian Queen* thought had disappeared. Unless the guy had a twin, it was him. "Do you mind if I send this to myself?" she asked.

"Be my guest."

Rachel tapped her cruise ship email address: RJP@security.coralqueen.com into Charlotte's phone and sent herself a copy of the photo before handing it back.

"I don't suppose you have any photos of Eleanor, do you?"

"Oh, I hadn't thought of that," she said. "Let me look."

"Right." Rachel waited again, only this time she sat back in her chair, mulling it over. She checked her notes from Jason's research, then she walked over to the desktop computer and checked. He had boarded under the same name – the name of an apparent ghost with no past. *Who is Sam Akbar? Supposedly dead and now alive. Why was he with Belinda Marlow?*

"Here we are," said Charlotte, clapping her hands together before handing her phone to Rachel, who sat down again.

Eleanor looked intense even at dinner. It must have been taken during the celebrity dinner from the night when Charlotte met her. "Was the man named Sam at the same dinner?"

Charlotte scratched her head. "Not that I saw. It was the first night aboard, and I only noticed him the second day after seeing Eleanor again. She wasn't big on conversation... or having her photo taken." Charlotte chuckled. "I snapped that when she wasn't looking."

The lighting in the photo was dim, but there was no doubting it was Eleanor. Charlotte had now produced photographic evidence of both, but doing what? Enjoying dinner and scowling. It wasn't much to go on.

Except for the man overboard fiasco. "Can I send this one to myself as well?"

"Please do," she said. "If I find any more later, I'll send them to the address you've tapped into my phone. I know how to send photos via email."

"Thanks," said Rachel. "That might be useful."

"And you don't know whether Sam Akbar—"

"I remember the name now," said Charlotte. "The guard who interviewed me pronounced it differently."

"Was he working with the celebrity chef on the previous cruise?"

"Not that I remember, although I didn't attend the auction evening. I only attended one dinner where the ticket money went to charity. You could ask Belinda Marlow whether he worked for her before. I didn't believe the randomly chosen thing. I'm so sorry for wasting your time, Rachel, telling you about his death that turns out wrong."

Rachel wished she could tell Charlotte that she wasn't wasting her time and that the man had been thought to go overboard. All this cloak-and-dagger stuff was confusing her. How are they getting away with it? The ship's security systems were stringent. Anyone boarding a cruise had to prove their identity beforehand. Could it be, as Tamara suggested, that the glitches were video blocking technology, or was it just plain old hacks? They had to have someone on the inside. And that someone had to be able to influence who boarded and exited the ship. She needed to speak to Bert Holland, the IT guy. He must be hiding something.

"I feel much better now, Rachel," said Charlotte, polishing off her drink. "I'm sorry for wasting your time, but thank you for looking after me. Something's happened to Eleanor though, hasn't it?"

Rachel said, "Why don't you get some rest? It was an awful night last night, and you've had a long day."

Charlotte gave Rachel a knowing look but didn't quiz her further. "Thank you. I expect you need to get back to that dinner," she said with a smile.

"I expect I do," said Rachel. "Are you sure you'll be all right? Would you like me to escort you to your room?"

"I'm better now. It was the shock. Now I know it was nothing, and that I was just being silly before. It's a relief. You know that 'do not disturb' sign on Eleanor's door is a dead giveaway?"

"You get some rest," Rachel said.

"I see, Mum's the word," she said as she left.

Rachel sat for a good five minutes after Charlotte had left. What the heck's going on? Was this night going to be as long as last night? Should she return to the VIP evening knowing it was expected of her? Too right, she should. She had to speak to Sam Akbar.

21

When Rachel got back to the restaurant, the auction was coming to an end, and people were starting to leave for the dance.

She observed Sam Akbar; her brief checks before leaving her office revealed he was travelling as an American. *Who are you, and what are you doing on board this ship?*

What did Belinda Marlow have to do with what had happened previously, and what was happening on board the *Coral Queen*? Watching them together, Belinda and Akbar seemed closer than random strangers. She caught Rosemary's eye and gave her a nod. The guests at her own table were still sitting there, so she headed back.

"Oh, hello, Chief. We thought we'd lost you," said Charles. "I wish you'd stayed; you might have saved me a fortune. I've gone and bought one of the places to cook with Belinda."

Rachel grinned. "I'm sure you'll enjoy it. Sounds like a marvellous opportunity, and judging by the food tonight, you'll pick up some amazing new skills."

"You're quite right, of course. I do like to dabble in a bit of entertaining myself."

Rachel enjoyed the interlude of conversation around the table, mainly sitting back and listening, but her eyes drifted towards Sam Akbar. She wished she could tell Jason and interview the death-defying Sam Akbar. Did he survive going overboard, or was it a ruse? Initially, she had wanted to confront him, but now felt the better play would be to observe. Observation was key in situations like this because notifying him that she knew what had happened previously would make him clam up. He could even disappear again. She wondered if Akbar and Belinda were in a relationship, but from what she saw, theirs was a professional partnership. It struck her that maybe Charlotte was right and that he was Eleanor's ex. Was that why he watched her on the previous cruise? Or was it to do with her job? Did he kill her?

Rachel was beginning to wonder if this was a lot simpler than it first appeared. Except that Eleanor had been able to get around the IT and security systems, not to mention boarding the ship willy-nilly, cloning access cards, and posing as crew.

Chapter 21

As more people started to move for the after-dinner dance, Rachel said goodnight to those at her table and sidled next to Rosemary.

"Anything?"

"Alex said he hadn't seen anything or anyone he recognised and was pleased to be given permission to leave. I can't see why Eleanor would pick him to work with, if I'm honest."

"Maybe she needed his hacking skills. What about that man?"

"Apart from him being a good salesman and appearing to be on Belinda's payroll by the way he eked money out of people, no. Who is he?"

"His name is Sam Akbar, and he's a person of interest," she whispered.

"What happened to the lady you left with?"

"That was Charlotte Kieft. She's fine, but it was she who alerted me to that man. He's supposed to be dead."

Rosemary's jaw dropped. "You mean the man Jason was looking into?"

"From the *Meridian Queen*. Yes. Jason found nothing on him except that he had travelled previously under a US passport, he went missing just like Charlotte told me, and was presumed to have gone overboard while coincidentally there was another glitch in the CCTV at the time."

"How the heck is he avoiding our systems picking these things up?" Rosemary's eyes were wide.

"That's what we need to find out. There must be someone on the inside, maybe in the IT team."

"He's quite the ladies' man. He managed to charm a lot of money out of people. Not that they can't afford it," said Rosemary. "And it's all going to a good cause. Belinda Marlow's really popular. What was the food like?"

Rachel licked her lips. "It was delicious and worth attending for; Belinda's an excellent chef."

"And what did our chefs say about her?" Rosemary asked.

"They like her; none of them had a bad word to say about her. She's professional, and her PA manages access and everything. I'd almost discounted her until Akbar turned up."

"Is Charlotte sure it's the same man?"

Rachel took out her phone, opening the email with the photo taken on board the *Meridian Queen*. Rosemary enlarged it just as Rachel had done, inspecting it closely.

"It's him," she said.

"Look at the next one," said Rachel.

Rosemary opened the next email to see the photo of Eleanor. She zoomed in on that and inspected it. "Different hairstyle and colour, but yeah, that's Eleanor from the post-mortem photos."

"I'll send these to Jason and let him know what we've got."

"What have we got?" asked Rosemary.

"Not a lot on its own, but putting it together we have a man who was behaving suspiciously on the previous cruise and appeared to be watching Eleanor. Charlotte assumed he was an ex and that Eleanor got rid of him. Now he's here. His arrival on a ship where Eleanor ends up dead is our only lead."

"Apart from the video blocking thing Tamara mentioned," said Rosemary.

"Which could turn out to be plain old tampering. We really haven't got enough evidence on that."

"But the blackout?"

Rachel wished she could tell Rosemary the full story, as it could be linked, especially if Sam Akbar turned out to be an American spy or double agent. "Let's focus on this man for now. I'd like to speak to him, but I don't want him to know we're on to him. We need to follow him and see what he's up to."

"Do you want me on it, boss?"

"Yes, but Rosemary, be discreet. If this guy managed to disappear and reappear and has no past..."

"I get it. He could be a foreign agent. Are we going to bring Tamara in at this stage and get her to gather CCTV footage of him?"

"We do need to gather the CCTV," said Rachel, "but first I want to speak to the IT chief and see what's going on there. Do you know anything about his wife's death?"

"All I know is that it was odd."

"Odd, how?" asked Rachel.

"She was given the wrong dose of a drug in Switzerland, of all places. I mean, the Swiss; their systems are incredible. I'm not saying mistakes couldn't happen there, but I did some cold-water slalom training in the country, and everything is digitalised."

Rachel felt a cold sweat dripping down her back. "We seem to have a lot of computer glitches revolving around our ship and now its crew. They're all linked somehow. I wonder if there's a way we can get hold of his wife's records?"

"Dr Bentley would be the best person to ask about that. Jason says he's got contacts all over the world. And if he tells the hospital it's relevant to the late Mrs Holland's husband's mental health, he might get access. Although you know what medics are like. Very protective of their records. Almost as protective as a priest."

"Either way, I'd like to try. I will see if there's an opening to speak to Bert Holland. We need to know if the two things are connected."

"How could they be? Surely if someone was threatening him, it would be in their interest to keep his wife alive."

"Does he have children?"

Rosemary stroked her chin. "I hadn't thought about that. Teenagers, from what I gathered. Jason said they've moved in with their aunt. Are you suggesting the wife's death was a warning and the teenagers are under threat?"

"It's a bit far-fetched," said Rachel. "But we have to know if he's clean and whether somebody is blackmailing or bribing him. I can't believe these people can get on and off the ship without having someone on the inside, and that someone has to be in IT."

"It could be someone at head office," said Rosemary.

"That's another thought," said Rachel. *Perhaps I should consider the head office's security chief who has got the cruise line on tenterhooks,* she thought. "And on that note, I'm going to get a good night's sleep and approach it fresh in the morning. Goodnight, Rosemary."

"See you tomorrow, Chief."

22

Rachel knew she had to bring Tamara Shutt into the loop but still hesitated over how much information to share. She decided not to mention Sam Akbar, although she couldn't work like this for long. Her desire to give the team the full picture and have them onside was overwhelming. Looking at everyone with suspicion didn't suit her; it was a horrendous position to be in.

Before heading to bed, Rachel had one more thing to do. She headed into the IT office. Bert Holland wasn't there, but his deputy, Fritz, was in his office. Rachel knocked and entered.

"Hello, Rachel, what brings you here?" he asked with a beaming smile. "Or need I ask after last night? I've just finished my checks and everything's going as it should. We've added an extra layer of security and limited access; thus far, there have been no glitches."

"Brilliant," said Rachel.

"I'm hoping what happened was a once-in-a-lifetime thing."

"Me too," said Rachel. "As I'm in the vicinity, I was hoping to catch a word with Bert. Is he around?"

"He left about an hour ago. He got a telephone call and told me he had to step out for a while."

"Did he say where to or who called?"

"Sorry, no. But from the way he spoke, I assume it's technical. He's been working closely with the engineering team today, so he could be there. He might even be on the bridge."

"Thanks for that," said Rachel.

"Do you want me to call him?"

"No thanks," said Rachel. "It's not urgent. I'll catch him tomorrow." As she left, Rachel had no intention of waiting until tomorrow, but she didn't want to make Fritz suspicious. She headed down to the security office to check the CCTV. From there, she could monitor screens all over the ship, including the bridge and engineering, not to mention kitchens and other areas; they had access to everything.

"Hello, boss," said Ravanos, moving aside to let her scan. "Are you looking for anything in particular?"

"Yes, I want to speak to Bert Holland. Have you seen him?"

Ravanos stroked his chin. "I did see him; let me think. Now, where was it?" He scrunched his eyes.

Rachel waited while he thought. He was a good officer, not the sharpest in the team but reliable and trustworthy. He didn't shoot his mouth off.

"Oh, I know where it was. He and Aryna were in the buffet grabbing a bite to eat."

Rachel switched screens to the buffet and caught a shot of them sitting at a dining table in deep conversation. "Thanks, have a good night." Rachel left Ravanos to his duties and took the stairs. She hadn't been for a run or to the gym, having been on duty more or less since the storm hit in the middle of the night. She craved exercise normally but had been running on adrenaline all day. The lavish dinner had left her feeling sluggish, so an extra burst of adrenaline might wake her up. She took the steps two at a time up eight flights to deck twelve before entering the buffet. The food aromas made her feel queasy. Perhaps it hadn't been such a good idea to run up so many flights of stairs after a heavy meal. Her stomach was complaining about the need for time to digest. She slowed her pace and poured herself a glass of water from a drinks machine before heading to where she had seen Bert and Aryna from the monitor.

The two officers were locked in conversation at the same table. The buffet was otherwise quiet. Most guests were enjoying evening entertainment or having early nights after the storm.

Bert's eyes widened with fear when he looked up at her. Aryna's were more hostile. She approached casually.

"Hello," she said, opting for a disarming smile. "I was so hoping to find you up here. Do you mind if I join you?" Neither answered, but she sat down anyway. "I was hoping for a catch-up."

Aryna's eyes narrowed. "Nothing's changed since you called earlier. We have done nothing wrong. Whatever happened has got nothing to do with engineering."

"It remains a mystery," Rachel replied, taking a sip of water. "I just wondered if anything else had come to your notice. Anything out of the ordinary today?"

Aryna shook her head. "Not in engineering. We've checked every system for flaws and irregularities, but we cannot find out what happened during the night. It must have been a rare phenomenon from the lightning strike rather than anything else. We don't have saboteurs in engineering."

"No-one said anything about saboteurs, but I'm glad to hear it," said Rachel with a smile.

Aryna forced a smile, but it didn't reach her eyes. "If you'll excuse me, I need to get back to work. I'm relieving my deputy tonight, just to make sure nothing else is going to go wrong."

"That's very conscientious of you," said Rachel.

"It's my job," snapped Aryna, with a serious glare.

Rachel watched the senior engineer stomp out of the buffet.

"Don't mind her. She's been insecure ever since Russia became persona non grata. You know how it is."

"Not really," said Rachel. "We're one nation on this ship, and I don't judge people based on their nationality, whether I agree with what their governments are up to or not."

"Me neither," said Bert. "Although not everyone sees it that way."

"Let me know if there's anyone I need to speak to about that," said Rachel. "Captain Jenson made it clear to me when I took this job that his policy is one of inclusion." Rachel recalled the conversation where he had told her she had to make the judgement calls between free speech and intolerance.

"Sure," said Bert, shifting in his seat as if about to get up.

"Before you leave, would you mind if I ask you a few questions?" said Rachel.

Bert's body language changed immediately, becoming more defensive. "Sure, go ahead."

"Now, I'm not saying this happened; I'm just asking if this could happen. Is it possible for somebody in IT to override safety mechanisms that would cause a blackout like we had last night?"

Chapter 22

"The problem isn't in IT, I'm telling you. If it was a hack, it came from somewhere else."

"Okay," said Rachel, "let's forget about last night. I wanted to ask you about something else entirely."

"Oh," said Bert, folding his arms.

"Is it possible for somebody in IT to bring or allow a person on board the ship without it going through official channels?"

Bert's brow furrowed before he looked up at her. "Anything's possible with digital technology nowadays. But our staff are carefully screened before boarding. They each have their own jobs. The only people who would have that kind of access would be me and my deputy. What about someone from your team? That seems more likely to me."

That was also a possibility in Rachel's mind, but she didn't want to go there yet. "Could someone employed to do something else be able to override the system?"

"In order to answer that question, I'd need you to be a bit more specific," said Bert.

"If, for example, there was a person on a cruise – not this one – but a person on another cruise who went missing, and this person's disappearance was reported and investigated, but no trace of their existence was found, and they later turned up on another cruise, what I want to know is whether someone like that could board this ship, for instance, without help from the inside?"

"Oh, I see what you're getting at," said Bert. "You mean an insider would have to approve them. But that's not the only case. If there was a hack, it could come from anywhere in the world and we might not know about it. Russia or China have the capability, along with the usual suspects in the Middle East or a rogue state. Good hackers can infiltrate any system to get one of their people on board if they really want to. I'm sure it happens more often than we'd like to think."

"Oh," said Rachel, "that wasn't quite the answer I was hoping for."

"When I say it happens, I'm sure it doesn't occur all the time, but I guess it could if someone was determined enough. We all know, Rachel, that countries have ways of getting foreign nationals into places they shouldn't be. That said, our systems are rigid, as you well know, being chief of security, so they would have to be exceptionally good at what they do. If you're referring to someone causing the blackout last night, I'd go back to whether there's an insider in your department."

Rachel swallowed hard. She just didn't want to think about it but Bert was on a roll. "It would be harder to come from IT because such a person would need extensive knowledge of how to hide their digital footprint. Whereas one of your guys or gals could let the person on board, knowing they needed to be invisible."

"But no-one in my team would have the knowledge to do what happened last night," she said.

"Maybe someone working for a rogue state did that." Bert seemed to enjoy seeing her squirm.

"I don't believe anyone could infiltrate our systems from outside, but if you can find anything that points to an outside hack, please let me know about it." Now it was his turn to look uncomfortable.

"We've been looking at it all day and can't find anything."

A dirty security guard could have deliberately overlooked or even facilitated minor hacks. Rachel breathed out a heavy sigh, hoping a member of her team wasn't involved. There might be some bad eggs, but they'd been with the cruise line for a long time. She couldn't see them doing something like this, but maybe one of the new ones. She tried a different tack. "I was sorry to hear about your wife. I didn't realise until today."

"Yeah, well. These things happen." He looked down.

"Do you know how the mistake happened?" asked Rachel.

"I'd rather not talk about it," said Bert, standing up. "If that's all the questions, Rachel, I'd better get back."

"Thanks for your help." Rachel watched the troubled man leave. Was he a grieving husband, a traitor, or a man under threat? She had to find out.

23

The ship dropped anchor in Nuuk early. Rachel had managed a few hours' sleep in between her deliberations but got up early, hoping that Eleanor's planned meetings would provide the leads she needed.

Sarah was pacing the floor like a caged beast that had been released. Her enthusiasm was contagious.

"People would think you've been locked away for weeks, the way you're behaving."

Sarah giggled. "That's how it feels, but I'm so excited about our day out. Jason expressed reservations this morning, so I shot off while he was in the shower."

Rachel couldn't resist laughing, although she had her own reservations about having Sarah along. "Come on then. Let's go before I get a call."

They were casually dressed in jeans and jumpers suited to the weather. Rachel had a puffer jacket over her clothes and wore sturdy shoes. Sarah was wearing a thick duffle coat. They climbed into the tender that would take them to shore.

With a tender full of excited passengers, Rachel and Sarah kept their conversation casual to avoid drawing attention to themselves. A few passengers recognised Sarah and thanked her for treating their injuries, each wanting to give her a report on how they were. Sarah patiently listened while Rachel mulled over the possibilities of having a traitor on board the *Coral Queen*. It had been late when she went to bed the night before, so she hadn't followed up on Bert's wife's death. The more she thought about it, the more she felt that, in light of what was happening on board, the death was suspicious. Rachel fired a quick text to Jason to ask him to speak to Graham Bentley about obtaining the medical records.

By the time they reached the pier, Sarah's patients leapt up and disembarked with surprising agility. Sarah and Rachel were the last to leave, politely waiting for the other passengers to disembark. Once they were at the end of the pier, Rachel saw a sign with Eleanor's name on it.

"There," she pointed.

They approached the man holding the sign and handed over the ticket.

"I was told one passenger," the beefy man with shoulder-length sandy hair that fell around his shoulders, said gruffly. His bushy beard and moustache covered his mouth as he spoke.

"It was originally, but I brought a friend along," said Rachel, hoping to sound casual. "We'll still do exactly what you were hired for."

"If you say so." The man's eyes were as cold as the chilly wind. He climbed into the front seat of an SUV with all-weather tyres. The interior was slightly worn, showing frequent use in the harsh climate. Privacy glass separated him from his passengers as they took their seats in the rear. As soon as they were inside, the doors locked automatically. Sarah's anxious green eyes fixed on Rachel's.

Rachel forced a smile. "It's okay," she said in a low voice. Inwardly, she hoped their phone trackers would at least give Jason some idea of where they were heading.

The man drove in silence. It wasn't long before they left the urban landscape and were surrounded by stunning, yet raw, nature. The road wound through the terrain, with cliffs bordering them on the left and the icy waters of a fjord on the right. Sarah seemed to forget her apprehension, snapping photos of the fjord instead.

Rachel looked ahead with each turn, seeing towering snow-capped mountains in the distance. September marked the end of summer for Greenland, and the colours were already shifting to reds and oranges as autumn approached. The air inside the taxi was crisp and cool. They passed a few turf houses similar to those she had seen on a visit to the Norwegian countryside a few years before.

Once Sarah stopped snapping pictures, she cast an anxious glance at Rachel. Rachel was aware they were driving into the unknown, and she shared her friend's apprehension. She smiled reassuringly. Their glance raised unspoken questions that hung in the air: Where were they going, and who were they going to meet?

As they continued the journey into the wilderness, the only sound was the hum of the engine. Rachel took a sip of water from the bottle in her rucksack, wishing it was coffee to soothe her rapidly drying mouth.

The tension in the taxi eased when Sarah gasped, pointing to a herd of reindeer grazing in a meadow. "Look over there." She removed her camera once more.

"Gorgeous," said Rachel, wishing she could enjoy what, on any other occasion, would be an adventurous and enjoyable journey. She had read in the literature before the storm that they might see arctic foxes, seals, and whales during the cruise. If only she wasn't dealing with a murder and spy stuff.

After around thirty minutes, the driver turned along a dirt track in the middle of nowhere. Rachel could feel her heart rate increasing but focused on the green and hardy plant life, which helped ease her growing anxiety. They had driven for a mile when the SUV pulled up in front of a timber cottage next to a small lake.

Much to Rachel's relief, she heard the click of the passenger doors as they were unlocked. The driver said nothing. Sarah was out of the car before Rachel had time to assess whether they were walking into a trap.

Perhaps Jason's doubts about bringing Sarah along after what she'd suffered the day before were right. But it was too late now. She climbed out slowly, hoping her defensive skills would be enough if the situation turned out to be dangerous. The driver stayed where he was, and the much cooler air hit Rachel. She pulled her coat tighter, focusing on the charming cottage facing them, with its sloping grass and moss-covered roof blending into its surroundings. Sarah put her arm through Rachel's as they walked towards the only building. "It's beautiful."

"Are you okay?" Rachel asked.

"Sure. Being driven into the middle of nowhere by a silent gorilla is my idea of the perfect day out."

Rachel appreciated the attempt at humour, but concern for her friend made her nervous. They were isolated and vulnerable. She could have kicked herself for embarking on this mission. "Would you rather wait outside?"

"Not with a man who looks like the baddie from a James Bond movie. No."

Rachel squeezed Sarah's hand, took a breath, and knocked on the door. A woman in her sixties opened it. She didn't look threatening, but Rachel's senses were on high alert. The woman stared up at Rachel with sharp grey eyes and then scrutinised them both. "You're not Eleanor."

"Do you mind if we come inside?"

"Not until you tell me who you are."

Rachel removed the ID card from her inner coat pocket. "I'm Rachel Jacobi-Prince, chief of security on board the *Coral Queen*. This is Sarah Goodridge-Bradshaw, a nurse from the ship. If Eleanor is a friend, I'm afraid we have some bad news."

The woman was around five feet six with light dyed brown hair. She spoke with an English accent. Her features were as sharp as her eyes, and there was a world-weary air about her. She said something in an unfamiliar language and waved the driver back as he suddenly appeared behind them, most likely wondering why they weren't going inside.

"Okay. Come in."

Rachel and Sarah followed the woman, who hadn't yet given her name, inside. The cottage's decor had a homely feel, but a damp smell suggested it wasn't being lived in. Perhaps it was a safe house or a meeting place.

"What language was that you spoke just now?" Sarah asked.

"Greenlandic," their host replied. "Most of the population has adopted it as the official language. It's a form of rebellion against the Danes, but many people speak Danish." They stepped inside a cosy room with a crackling fire in a fireplace against one wall. The flickering flames cast a glow and provided them with warmth. Rachel didn't sense anybody else in the building, and she relaxed.

"What's happened to Eleanor?" The woman didn't appear to be one for chitchat.

"I'm sorry to inform you," said Rachel. "Eleanor Brodie's body was discovered in the ship's laundry in the early hours of yesterday morning. I'm trying to find out who is responsible, so I'm following up on every lead. She had a ticket for a private tour, which I gave to your driver, and here we are."

"Here you are indeed," said the woman, not flinching at the news. "How did she die?"

"Her neck was broken," said Rachel, seeing no point in lying to whoever this woman was. "Do you mind telling me who you are? And what your relationship was with Eleanor?"

"We worked together, that's all."

Another spy, thought Rachel, noting she didn't give her name. "Were you still working together?"

The woman sighed as she crossed the wooden planks, which creaked slightly underfoot. She took a seat in an armchair, indicating for Rachel and Sarah to sit. "No, we weren't. Eleanor said she had something to show me."

Rachel and Sarah sat on a sofa with a coffee table between them and Eleanor's aloof former colleague.

"May I ask what your background is?"

"That's a good question," said the woman, assessing Rachel. Her eyes were intense as she kept one eye on the door. She didn't trust them.

Rachel explained, "I've discovered that Eleanor found out something, which I assume is what she wanted to show you. Do you have any idea what it was?"

The woman still didn't reply.

"It would help if I knew your area of expertise."

"I was a cybersecurity expert, but I retired. I told Eleanor I wanted nothing to do with that sort of thing anymore, but she could be very persuasive. Plus, I owed her a favour. She saved my life a while back."

"We know she worked for British intelligence," said Rachel, noticing Sarah's jaw drop, but thankfully, she didn't comment.

"Eleanor no longer worked for British intelligence."

Now it was Rachel's turn to drop her jaw. "But I was told she did."

"Told by whom?" asked the woman.

"I'd rather not say unless you can help me," said Rachel. "Before I divulge any more information, I need you to tell me what she wanted you to look at."

"She said she'd found a flaw in your systems that someone was trying to sell. I believe it involved the ability to hack ship technology."

"Do you think that's possible?" asked Rachel.

"Anything's possible nowadays. Why do you think I

retired? I'd give anything for a quiet life, and I've got that here. I live in seclusion. Nobody knows about my past. Indeed, I have no past, and it suits me."

"I assume you have a name?" Rachel tried again.

"Carmen. It's not my real name, but I love the opera, so I call myself Carmen. Why don't I make us a hot mug of Greenland coffee while you decide whether you're going to tell me anything else? Either way, I don't mind. As I told you, I'm retired."

Carmen left the room, and Rachel could hear her moving around in the kitchen.

"You didn't tell me Eleanor Brodie was a spy," Sarah whispered.

"Sorry. I'm still not sure it's relevant," said Rachel, weighing up the ex-boyfriend theory alongside others.

"Do you trust her?" Sarah nodded towards the door, where Rachel heard the sounds of a coffee machine bubbling.

Rachel wasn't sure who to trust, but Eleanor had shared the information about the security flaw, and if she was going to move this case forward, she had to take a risk.

Carmen entered, carrying a tray of delicious-smelling coffee. Rachel made her decision. "Eleanor hired a hacker who believes she was working for MI6. He's an IT expert, but she kept him in the dark about her mission."

"That sounds like Eleanor. She got bitten and

Chapter 23

developed trust issues, which made her a maverick. It's probably what got her killed." Still no emotion was evident, just a resignation in Carmen's tone, the only hint at what she was feeling.

"All I know is that she was meeting someone in the early hours on the night she died," Rachel said, lifting the coffee mug and cupping it in her hands.

"In the laundry?" Carmen raised an eyebrow.

Rachel sighed. "I believe so, but whether that person killed her is what I'm trying to find out."

Carmen shook her head. "As far as I'm aware, Eleanor left the service. I assumed she was working privately."

"Who for?"

"In our line of work, we don't ask too many questions. She used to work for British intelligence but fell in love with a foreign agent. Although he claimed allegiance to a friendly country, it's still frowned upon. The fact that he had dual nationality with an unfriendly country made it all the more complicated. It's a dangerous business, falling in love."

Don't I know it, thought Rachel as she remembered her fiancé dumping her for another woman. She had found it difficult to trust anyone after that, and it had taken Carlos years to win her round. It had turned out well for her in the end, thanks to Carlos's patience. "Hence the trust issues, I suppose. Do you know the person's name?"

"I think you already know his name," Carmen answered.

Sarah was looking at both of them as if she were in a movie. "I have no idea what you two are talking about, so I'm going to enjoy this," she said, taking a huge gulp of coffee.

"Does the name Sam Akbar mean anything to you?" Rachel asked.

"Yes, he's the one she fell in love with; Iranian, American. She ended the relationship but had it bad. Until she called me a few weeks ago, I thought she was back home nursing a broken heart."

"And after she phoned, you thought she was working privately."

Carmen nodded. "It worried me when she told me what it was all about, because if she was going to sell to the highest bidder... well..."

Rachel wondered if Carmen meant what she thought she did. Things were starting to make sense.

24

Rachel cupped the exceptionally strong coffee between her palms, letting the warmth seep into her fingers. The bitter aroma filled her nostrils as she polished it off with a gulp, feeling the caffeine work its way through her system. It chased away the fatigue that threatened to overwhelm her.

"This coffee could strip paint," she remarked with a grin.

"Greenlanders like a strong blend. Besides, it's an old intelligence habit. Always be alert."

Rachel set the mug down on the crude wooden coffee table and unzipped her coat. The heat from the fire reminded her that the puffer coat was too thick for the room. With slightly trembling fingers, she reached into her inner pocket and retrieved the micro-SD card she had discovered in the early hours of the night before. An item so innocuous – a tiny rectangle that could fit on her fingernail – it was hard to imagine it might hold the key to unlocking a murder.

"This might be nothing," Rachel said, holding the card between her index finger and thumb, "but I found it after Eleanor's body was discovered." The memory of Eleanor's lifeless body crumpled on the sheet press sent an involuntary shiver down her spine. "We think the killer may have dropped it when escaping through a hatch leading to an underfloor tunnel from the laundry."

She placed the card in the centre of the table. "I haven't been able to open it, but it could be our only lead. The person Eleanor employed doesn't seem to know very much at all, and I haven't mentioned this to him yet."

Sarah shifted uncomfortably on the lumpy sofa beside her. Despite being a ship's nurse who had seen her share of trauma during previous adventures, she was clearly out of her depth. Rachel felt a pang of guilt for dragging her friend into this mess, but she trusted Sarah's judgement.

Carmen picked up the micro-SD card, examining it with a practiced eye.

"You think Sam Akbar killed her, don't you?" Carmen suggested, her tone casual but her eyes sharp as she studied Rachel's reaction.

Rachel measured her response. "Right now, all

options are open. He's one of several lines of inquiry and definitely a person of interest. I'm assuming he won't try to escape in Greenland as we've not let him know he's a person of interest."

"How did you find out about him?" Carmen asked, waving the card in the air. "He's a sneaky one. Few people could get to Eleanor, but he managed it."

"I found out through an unlikely source, actually," said Rachel, casting a sideways glance and winking at Sarah. "A woman with keen powers of observation remembered him and Eleanor from a previous cruise."

"Okay. Let me look at what you've got here." Carmen produced a laptop from a cupboard packed with biscuits. The incongruity almost made Rachel laugh. Here they were discussing murder and espionage, and Carmen kept her high-tech equipment hidden among treats.

Carmen opened the laptop and began a quiet tap-tap of keys. Rachel counted the seconds, aware of the pressure building behind her temples. Carmen inserted the card and typed a few commands before frowning. The light from the screen cast shadows on her face, making her look older.

"This is going to take a while; it's encrypted." Carmen's brow furrowed as she looked at the screen. "And the encryption's good. Eleanor was good at her job."

Rachel asked, a thought that had been nagging her

since Charlotte Kieft's revelation. "Could she have got back with Sam or switched sides?"

"Not as far as I know." Carmen continued tapping keys while speaking. "She broke it off when she got in too deep, even though she swore he was on a good side." The retired spy's mouth moved into a cynical smile. "Not that there is a good side these days. We're all as bad as each other."

"You might be right," said Rachel, though the notion that there were no good guys went against everything she believed in and troubled her deeply. "Do you think you'll be able to get into that?"

"It could take a few hours," said Carmen.

Rachel glanced at her watch.

"Is there somewhere else you need to be?" Carmen asked, noting the gesture.

"Eleanor had a lunch date, so I've only got about an hour." Rachel kept the urgency from her voice but felt time slipping away from her.

"I'll see what I can do." Carmen's expression softened slightly. "Why don't you go for a walk outside and leave me to concentrate? It's beautiful out there."

Rachel wasn't sure she wanted the disk out of her sight, but she was also under time pressure. The conflict must have shown on her face, because Carmen added, "I've been doing this since before you were born, Chief of Security Jacobi-Prince. Your disk is safe with me."

With a reluctant nod, Rachel motioned for Sarah to

follow, and they stepped outside into the cooler air of the Greenland autumn. After the warmth of the cottage, it was a shock. She zipped her coat up quickly.

As soon as they were outside, Sarah grabbed Rachel's arm. Her fingers dug into the thick fabric of her coat.

"What the heck is all this about?" Sarah's cheeks were red, whether from the cold or the shock of the clandestine meeting was difficult to tell.

"I'm as confused as you are." Rachel shook her head.

They began walking, their thick shoes crunching on the gravel. The surrounding landscape was a vast expanse of green, with autumnal colours intermingling with the wilderness. The snowcapped mountains remained visible in the distance.

"So, was Eleanor working for the British government or not?" Sarah asked, her voice sounding loud in the still air.

"That's now unclear. I thought she was. Alex told me she was." Rachel kicked a stone, sending it to join more of the same.

"Panicky Alex?"

"Yep. But after what Carmen said in there, Eleanor could have been lying to him," said Rachel. "Maybe she was working independently."

"What if she'd turned to some rogue state and Carmen didn't know?" Sarah suggested.

"That's unlikely but not impossible," Rachel

admitted, the words leaving a bitter taste in her mouth. Alex believed Eleanor was one of the good ones, and the fact she had arranged to meet Carmen suggested she was. "I wonder if her lunch date is Sam Akbar."

They walked towards the lake that stretched before them. Rachel imagined it would soon freeze over as the cold months approached. The driver appeared to be taking a snooze in the vehicle, his hat pulled down over his eyes.

"Speaking of lunch, she could have got a packet of those biscuits out while we waited." Sarah pulled her coat closer, the wind picking up as they walked.

Rachel smiled at her friend's practicality. Sarah needed to eat regularly, or her blood sugar would drop, so she could always be counted on to think about the essentials. "Maybe they are out of date. I can't believe Carmen lives in the cottage. It's more like a hideaway."

"Who is this Sam Akbar?" Sarah asked.

"You might not believe this, but he's supposed to be dead." Rachel watched Sarah's reaction carefully, noting the flash of disbelief.

"Oh my word." Sarah rolled her eyes dramatically as she bit her lip, the latter stress reaction so familiar that Rachel felt a rush of affection. "What on earth have you got into?"

"Hey, don't blame me. You found the body." Rachel chuckled, more as a sign of stress relief than humour.

"Strictly speaking, I examined the body," Sarah

corrected with mock seriousness, "and I'd like to point out that before you arrived, we'd never had a ship-wide blackout or found a dead spy in the laundry!"

Rachel grinned, grateful for the lightness. "So that's my fault too, is it?"

"No, but murder's bad enough without all this scary intrigue. Can't we call in the authorities or something?"

"Trust me, I'd like to, but in a situation like this, who do we trust?" Rachel looked at the blue sky. The answer to the question haunted her. "It's frustrating. There are so many lies; it's hard to fish out the truth." She kicked another stone, wishing it were as simple as calling in the local police. But nothing about this case was simple.

"The only reason we know about Sam Akbar at all is courtesy of Charlotte Kieft. She recognised him at the VIP dinner last night." Rachel shoved her hands deeper into her pockets. "He was supposed to have gone overboard on the *Meridian*'s maiden voyage. Jason looked into it and confirmed it, but the man was – or is – a ghost."

The wind picked up, and whistled around them. The cold was coming from the lake, stinging Rachel's cheeks. She turned her back on it and pulled up her hood to shield her face from the biting cold.

"I knew he was up to something yesterday," Sarah said, her nose red from the chill.

"This guy, Sam Akbar, was presumed to have gone overboard and didn't disembark; he turned out to be a person unknown," explained Rachel, the details still confusing. "But when Charlotte saw him last night at the dinner hosted by our very own celebrity chef, Belinda Marlow, it turns out he wasn't dead at all."

"But how can that happen?" asked Sarah, squinting as the sun emerged from behind a cloud.

"My question exactly." Rachel's foot caught on a stump of hardy grass, almost tripping her over. She regained her balance. "I don't know, but someone helped him, and I need to find out who."

"Was it Eleanor?"

"She was on the same cruise, but according to Charlotte, she suspected he was stalking Eleanor, so it must have been after the breakup." Rachel was still trying to put the pieces together in her mind. The timeline was too much of a coincidence not to be related, and relationships could be complicated.

"So he could have killed Eleanor," Sarah suggested.

"It's hard to know." Rachel pulled her hood tighter as the wind found its way through. "She obviously lied to Alex, but then she lies – or lied – for a living. Alex is convinced, if he's to be believed, that she's still working for British intelligence."

"But she could have still been working for the British and not told Carmen," Sarah pointed out.

"I suspect there's more than one person on the inside." Rachel stopped walking, turning to her friend. "Eleanor went to meet somebody in the early hours. We don't know whether that person is the one who killed her or whether it was someone else. Somebody is facilitating these people on and off the ship. And I suspect it's somebody from IT."

Sarah's eyes narrowed thoughtfully. "Bert Holland?"

"What makes you say that?" asked Rachel.

"He's been acting strange since his wife died." Sarah stamped her feet, trying to keep warm.

"I'm not surprised. It was a horrible thing to happen." Rachel recalled what she'd been told about the medical error.

"But he used to be so warm and friendly. I don't know whether he's still grieving, but he's not looking sad, and he's shiftier."

"Do you know him well?"

"No, but Bernard does. As you know, Bernard knows everybody." Sarah rubbed her gloved hands together. "And Bernard thinks he's up to something."

Rachel's heart sank at the thought that Bert Holland might be involved. She opened her mouth to respond when movement from the cottage caught her eye.

The door swung open, and Carmen waved them back inside. "Got it!" she called.

Relief surged through Rachel, followed by apprehension about what they might find. She and Sarah hurried back to the cottage, their footsteps in parallel.

25

As Carmen's driver navigated the winding road back into Nuuk, Rachel pressed her forehead against the cold glass, processing what Carmen had told them. Beside her, Sarah sat in equal silence, her usually excitable face solemn.

Rachel's mind was cataloguing suspects, motives, and evidence. Lord, give me wisdom, she prayed silently. It had become her reflex in moments like these, her quiet plea when investigating the depraved actions of humanity. Her faith had been challenged throughout her years as a serving homicide detective, but instead of turning away, it had become her anchor in the storms of chaos.

The driver slowed as they approached their destination, a charming, whitewashed building perched on the edge of the fjord. The Hotel Hans Egede stood out against the stark Greenland landscape. As they stepped out of the car, the biting wind whipped Rachel's hair across her face. The driver hadn't spoken and left without glancing back. A man of few words.

Sarah let out a low whistle as they entered the hotel lobby. Floor-to-ceiling windows showcased panoramic views of icy waters and towering cliffs. Rachel felt a momentary pang that they weren't here as tourists. Under different circumstances, she would have stopped to admire the stark beauty, even taking a photo to send to her parents and to Carlos.

"This place is special," Sarah said.

Rachel nodded, her mind focused on their purpose as she glanced at the internal plan. "The Sarfalik Restaurant's on the top floor," she said, checking her watch. According to what Rachel had discovered in Eleanor's room, the dead woman was meeting someone for lunch there. If this person wasn't her killer, they would show up soon.

"We need to hurry," she said when Sarah stepped into a lift queue. "We'll take the stairs." Sarah sighed but followed. Rachel would rather have been early, but they had to hope the person hadn't already arrived.

The restaurant was even more impressive than the lobby. While the structural elements featured simple Scandinavian design, the unobstructed view of the landscape beyond the windows was breathtaking. Natural light flooded the space, reflecting off the white tablecloths and polished silverware. The air carried the savoury aroma of fresh seafood and herbs that made Rachel's stomach grumble.

When Rachel and Sarah requested a table, not revealing anything about Eleanor's booking, they were shown to a simply set one near the window.

While Sarah chatted to a server, ordering coffee with her usual warmth, Rachel's eyes scanned the room. She noted exits, seated patrons, staff movements, and details, filing them away in her brain.

"There are three tables for two left," Rachel said, her gaze landing on one near the centre of the room. "That one over there has a reserved sign on it."

Sarah followed her line of sight. "That must be it, then." Her stomach let out an audible rumble, and she gave Rachel a pleading look. "Do you mind if we eat here, Rachel? I'm starving."

Rachel checked her watch again. There was time, and maintaining their cover as tourists was important. "Okay, but you order for both of us. I'll have fish."

Sarah's face brightened. "There's plenty to choose from," she said, eagerly scanning the menu.

The server returned with their coffees. Rachel feigned interest in her phone to discourage conversation from the friendly woman. Sarah, on the other hand, was happy to chat.

"This place is lovely," Sarah commented as the server placed their drinks on the table.

"The hotel's name translates as White Falcon in honour of the birds," the server replied, her English carrying a musical Nordic lilt. "You might see them soaring in the sky if you're lucky. Are you staying here?"

"No. We're from the *Coral Queen* cruise ship," Sarah explained, adding unnecessary details in Rachel's opinion. "We'll be leaving this evening and heading up the west coast."

"What a wonderful thing to do. I hope you enjoy Greenland. You've chosen the best time to visit."

Rachel sighed, wishing Sarah would end the small talk. Normally, she enjoyed friendly interactions, but right now, she had a job to do, and she needed to concentrate. Finally, the server left Sarah browsing the menu, much to Rachel's relief.

"Did I ever mention you're intense when you're working?" Sarah muttered over the top of her menu.

Rachel didn't reply, recognising the comment as one of Sarah's gentle attempts to lighten the mood. The restaurant had filled quickly, and the ambient noise of conversation and cutlery against plates grew louder.

And then, Rachel's breath caught in her throat as a man arrived. Opposite her, Sarah's mouth gaped open. The man they saw speaking to the head waiter was not Sam Akbar, as Rachel had been expecting, but a familiar face that sent a jolt of anger through her system.

Her heart thumped against her ribcage as anger rose

inside her. Wanting to be certain this wasn't a mistake, she hesitated to confront him. He looked around the room, and she raised her menu to obscure her face. Sarah followed suit. They watched as the man was shown to the reserved table. He ordered something, and shortly afterwards, a server placed a glass of beer in front of him. The server was dismissed with an impatient wave of his hand.

"That's—" Sarah began, her voice a shocked whisper.

"I know," interrupted Rachel, her voice tight. "Don't let him see us, or he'll run."

Clint Foster. One of her own security officers. The revelation hit Rachel as hard as a physical blow.

At that moment, the server distracted them, returning to take their orders. Rachel barely registered the exchange as Sarah ordered grilled Arctic char for both of them. The server mentioned something about reindeer being the local speciality, but Sarah loved the animals and couldn't bring herself to eat it.

While they waited for their lunch, Sarah tried to make small talk, but Rachel was too focused on Clint to engage. She could feel anger building in her chest until she thought her heart might explode. She forced herself to take deep, measured breaths.

Clint was supposed to be on duty, checking passengers on and off the tenders. He waited for twenty minutes, checking his watch several times. Rachel observed him with narrowed eyes, grateful now that Peter Jenson had instructed her to keep Eleanor's death a secret from all but a select few. If Clint had known, he wouldn't be sitting here, waiting for a woman who would never arrive.

Their food arrived, the aroma distracting Rachel from her surveillance for a moment. The Arctic char was beautifully presented, garnished with local herbs and accompanied by roasted vegetables. Under normal circumstances, Rachel would have appreciated the meal, as she was as enthusiastic about good food as she was about her fitness regime.

"What does he have to do with all this?" Sarah whispered across the table.

Rachel's eyes narrowed as she stabbed at her fish with more force than necessary. "I don't know, but I'm going to find out as soon as we get back to the ship. We have no authority here, and other than skiving, I've got nothing to accuse him of. We'll let him go."

They ducked their heads as Clint finished his beer and spoke to the server again. From this distance, Rachel couldn't hear the exchange, but the body language was clear enough.

"He's probably asking whether he's missed his lunch date," said Sarah, her fork paused halfway to her mouth as she resumed eating.

It was hard to imagine anyone being Clint's date. Not because of his size – though he was a bear of a man

– but because of his brusque demeanour. Still, he'd been married twice, Rachel reminded herself, although she suspected this lunch meeting was more business than pleasure.

The server shook his head, and Clint stood up, his expression a mix of confusion and irritation. He glanced around the room once more. Rachel bent down, pretending to tie her shoelaces, while Sarah positioned her menu to shield her.

"Do you think he saw us?" asked Sarah.

"I don't think so," said Rachel, straightening up once Clint left.

"Is it worth following him?" Sarah looked longingly at the remaining food on her plate.

Rachel shook her head. "No, let's eat lunch. He'll go back to the ship." She speared another piece of fish, her appetite returning now that the immediate threat of discovery had passed. "He was meeting Eleanor. That's all we know for certain."

"Why?"

"I don't know," Rachel admitted, "but I wonder if Belinda Marlow's a part of this. He gave her behind-the-scenes access without asking me." Rachel tried to enjoy the delicious meal that was to be savoured, but beneath her composed exterior, she was seething.

"Belinda seems too nice to be involved in spiery," said Sarah, stumbling over the word.

"I don't think there's such a word," said Rachel with a smile.

"You know what I mean." Sarah waved her fork in the air. "At least he's not a murderer because he doesn't know she's dead." Sarah's ability to look on the bright side was one thing Rachel most admired about her friend.

"You're right, but he's got to be our inside leak." A wave of self-recrimination washed over her. "I hate to think the traitor's in my team and I missed it."

"You're still new, Rachel," Sarah reminded her gently. "And you were already on to him, in a way. It wouldn't have taken you long to suss it out."

Rachel was sure that was true, but she'd been betting on someone on Bert's team, if not Bert himself, after what Sarah had been told by Bernard. "Maybe," she said.

"Do you think Clint was who Eleanor planned to meet in the laundry?"

"I doubt it. I've got a feeling that might have been Sam Akbar."

"But he wouldn't have access," said Sarah.

"Good point," said Rachel, acknowledging the fact. "But remember Eleanor cloned my access card. It could also have been Belinda Marlow; she was in the vicinity." *Or Bert Holland,* she thought, but didn't say aloud. "There's still somebody we haven't discovered."

She took a sip of water, the coolness clearing her mind. The pieces were there, but not fitting into place yet. Rachel needed more information and more evidence. Back home, she would have had a team of detectives to delegate to, forensic resources, databases. Here, because of the need to keep things quiet, she had a few trusted team members and Sarah. She remembered samples would be sent for forensics in Nuuk today, but had little hope they would lead to their killer.

"Well, I wish you'd find out soon, because all this cloak-and-dagger stuff is too much for me." Sarah polished off the rest of her meal. "Especially when I've got a pounding headache."

Rachel's focus shifted from the case to her friend's wellbeing. "Is it from the head injury?" Rachel asked, concerned. "You should tell Graham."

"No way; he'll make me have more time off. It's most likely low blood sugar. I'll be better now that I've eaten."

Rachel wasn't convinced, but knew better than to argue with Sarah about medical matters. Instead, she reached for her phone. "What say I call Jason and ask him to keep a watch on Clint while we do something touristy after lunch?"

"Like what?" Sarah asked, her lips forming a hopeful pout that reminded Rachel of their childhood days when Sarah would have to be prised away from her studying to go on an adventure.

"How about whale watching?" Rachel suggested,

knowing it was something Sarah had been keen to do since they learned about their Greenland itinerary.

"Now that I would love," said Sarah, her face lighting up. "Are you sure?"

Rachel would rather have headed straight back to the ship to throw Clint in the brig, but seeing the light return to Sarah's green eyes, she couldn't deny her. Her friend had already suffered on this cruise trying to help Rachel; she deserved some joy.

"It's the least I can do after putting you through a morning of spiery," Rachel said with a grin, adopting Sarah's made-up word.

They shared a moment of genuine laughter before settling the bill and heading out to where the boats took tourists on whale-watching trips.

26

After arriving back on board the *Coral Queen*, Rachel hugged Sarah. "Thanks for helping take my mind off things."

"The pleasure was all mine," said Sarah, beaming.

It had been a pleasant interlude, made even more rewarding when they saw several humpback whales during their boat trip. But now it was back to work. The respite had been necessary, yet now that she was back on board, the responsibilities returned.

She headed straight for her office, the familiar corridors of the ship providing some comfort, albeit now tainted by the knowledge that at least one traitor walked among them. Her phone was in her hand before she even reached the door. She pressed Jason's number.

"Where are you?" she asked.

Chapter 26

"Just heading your way. Sarah told me you were back."

Rachel contacted the bridge but was informed that Peter Jenson was on shore leave and would be back in an hour. That part of her mission would have to wait.

Moments later, she and Jason were in Rachel's office with mugs of coffee from the coffee machine on the table. The aroma added a satisfying familiarity, helping to clear her head. The day had been an emotional roller coaster. Rachel chose one of the comfortable chairs rather than the one behind her desk. This wasn't about hierarchy; she and Jason needed to think as equals. Jason sat in another chair, his posture straight and slightly tense.

"Have you seen Sarah?" she asked.

She noticed the flicker of concern crossing his face at the mention of his wife's name. "Briefly. She said your outing on land was a success, and I'm pleased my wife arrived back safely. Thanks for taking her on the whale watch. She's in her element."

Rachel laughed, the sound feeling out of place but helpful under the circumstances. "She deserved it after our interesting encounter with another spy, albeit a retired one. I think she's over yesterday's incident."

"That's good to hear," said Jason, his face reddening. The colour rising to his cheeks betrayed the depth of emotion he was trying to contain. "It's been hard to take. I don't know what I'd do without her."

Rachel understood that vulnerability all too well. She'd felt it herself when they found Sarah the day before, and the thought of losing someone you love could be paralysing. She was pleased Jason felt comfortable enough to share his feelings. "You're a good husband, but you need to trust her. Sarah's stronger than you give her credit for."

"I know, but she's also a tender soul." Jason's voice cracked as he added, "Sometimes I wonder if her mum's right and we should settle in England."

Rachel was fully aware of how much pressure Mary Bradshaw exerted on the couple to live what she called a normal life. But she really didn't want to think about that just now. It was selfish, but she'd like them to stay for the duration of her tenure as chief of security. The idea of them leaving was a bridge to cross another day. Right now, they had a murder to solve.

"We saw humpback whales," she said, deliberately steering the conversation into safer waters.

Jason grinned, the smile reaching his eyes and, for the moment, banishing the shadows there. "She sent some photos. You guys were lucky."

"It couldn't be all work, and it did us both good to get some chill time. And boy, was it chilly." The memory of the wind making her coat feel inadequate made her shudder.

Jason laughed before his face turned serious, a transformation Rachel was getting used to. It was the soldier in him, the ability to focus on the mission. "I kept an eye on Clint like you asked. He's been at his post all afternoon. Did Eleanor's meetings give us any leads?"

Rachel took a sip of coffee and leaned forward. "The first one led to a meeting with a woman who calls herself Carmen. Not her real name."

"Of course not," said Jason with a cynical smile.

"Carmen said that Eleanor was no longer working for MI6. Carmen herself is a retired cybersecurity expert and got into the micro-SD card." Rachel paused for a moment. "I assume the killer was disturbed by Manuel Campos, the laundry worker, and in a rush to escape, must have dropped the card in the tunnel. It revealed the vulnerability in cruise ship systems and other secret information, including a dossier on former agents."

She watched Jason's expression. His eyes narrowed enough to let her know he was processing the implications.

"Carmen couldn't be sure whether Eleanor had switched sides," Rachel continued, "but as I think Eleanor wanted to share what was on the disk with her, I doubt it. Carmen remains loyal to the British government and admitted Eleanor would only want to show her the contents if she was doing it for good."

"Unless she was only going to discuss the vulnerability and not the rest of it," said Jason.

Rachel rubbed her temples. "It's hard to know what

Eleanor was up to. I don't want to tackle state secrets or spy dossiers, but I want to know whether it was the reason someone killed her. Carmen removed and kept the secret spy stuff and gave me back the card containing the relevant vulnerability information to pass up the chain of command. I'll take it to Peter once we've finished."

Jason's eyebrows shot up. "Was it wise letting her have everything else? Can you trust her?"

Rachel had asked herself the same thing since leaving Carmen. "I think so. She was gutted at the thought of Eleanor working off the grid. Plus, I didn't want to test her mettle." A shiver ran through her as she recalled Carmen's hard eyes when she had put the proposal to Rachel. "She was helpful but battle-hardened. We might not have got out of there alive if I'd insisted on keeping it. Her driver was like hired muscle. I wouldn't have wanted to take him on, and I wouldn't be surprised if both he and Carmen had access to firearms."

"Oh, right." Jason's voice was flat but understanding. He'd seen combat and had friends who hadn't come back from war.

"Carmen confirmed Charlotte's theory that Sam Akbar was Eleanor's ex." Rachel swirled the remaining coffee in her mug, watching it form a dark whirlpool. "However, Eleanor ended the relationship when she felt she was getting in too deep with a fellow agent, although he was working for the Americans. I wonder if they rekindled the relationship after she left MI6."

Jason polished off his own coffee before looking up. "Rosemary looked him up. He's still travelling under an American passport. Other than that, I imagine the home details are fiction just like before."

"When Eleanor first met him, she could have been playing him but then fell in love." Rachel sighed. "As you discovered, he went dark until he turned up on our ship. We don't know why that was. I was convinced it was him Eleanor meant to have lunch with today, but it wasn't."

"It's enough to make your head spin," said Jason, running a hand through his hair. The military cut was one of the few visible reminders of his past service. Carlos had also been in the military, and he and Jason shared memories of their separate but familiar pasts.

Rachel nodded before adding a complexity she was wrestling with. "Another thing Sarah mentioned is that Bert Holland has been acting weird."

"I didn't think Sarah knew him that well."

"She doesn't, but Bernard does, and Bernard notices everything about everyone." Rachel smiled at the thought of the Filipino nurse who made it his business to be the ship's jester but who the crew opened up to. "I guess he's been keeping an eye out for him since his wife died. He'd be concerned for that reason, but he thinks Bert's up to something."

"Graham has agreed to find out what he can about Bert's wife's demise, but only because I said you thought it might have something to do with our case."

Dr Graham Bentley was nothing if not professional. It was a relief to have him onside. "I'm wondering if Bert Holland might be another insider."

"Another insider. How many have we got?" Jason asked.

Rachel took a deep breath before delivering the bombshell. "The reason I asked you to monitor Clint is that he turned out to be the man who arrived at Eleanor's lunch for two today."

Jason flopped back in his chair, genuine shock registering on his face. "Scumbag, how did he get off shift without me knowing about it?"

"That's what we're going to ask him, but not yet." Rachel's mind was racing. "We need to know where Belinda Marlow fits into all this, seeing as he gave her unrestricted and unsupervised access behind the scenes."

"I knew Clint was bad news, but I didn't imagine for one minute he'd be a traitor." Jason's eyes hardened. She recognised the controlled fury she herself had felt. "What do we do now?"

"My first instinct was to confront him, throw him in the brig, and have him fired, but while he thinks he's beyond suspicion, I suggest we follow our leads and set some traps. Let's get Rosemary and Ravanos in to discuss it."

As Jason reached for his radio to summon the others, Rachel was planning. At least the vulnerability issue could be resolved as soon as Peter came back from shore leave. He could get head office to fix it and do whatever they needed to do to prevent it from happening again. She exhaled. And it wouldn't be sold to the highest bidder. She had Eleanor and Carmen to thank for that. But there were still people who thought it was available, and she had to find them before anyone else was killed.

Rosemary and Ravanos joined Rachel and Jason in her office. As the door closed behind them,

Rachel met Jason's eyes, seeing her own determination reflected there. She outlined her plan.

27

Tamara Shutt had her eyes fixed on the CCTV when Rachel walked into the security team's office. The glow from the screen accentuated the dark circles under her eyes. It appeared she was determined to monitor the surveillance footage for as long as it took.

Rachel paused, observing Tamara. The woman's intensity put her on edge. There was something about her coiled alertness that reminded Rachel of a predator waiting to strike.

"Hi, how's it going?" Rachel kept her tone casual.

Tamara glanced up from her screen. "As well as can be expected. Everything's up and running with no further glitches here or in the main office. I've found a few more sightings of Eleanor, but not with anybody in particular."

Rachel moved to the monitors, maintaining a professional distance while looking over Tamara's shoulder. "Are there any of her with a dark-haired man, olive skin? He's American, Iranian?" Rachel asked, watching her reaction.

"No, is that something I should look for specifically?" Tamara tilted her head slightly to gain eye contact.

"Possibly. I just wanted to know if anything jumped out at you." Rachel remained unwilling to tell her about Sam Akbar.

Tamara's lips tightened into a thin line. "Nothing. She seemed aware of where the security cameras were and avoided them unless doing normal passenger activities like going for meals. That woman wasn't stupid."

Rachel nodded, contemplating conducting a trawl of Sam Akbar and Belinda Marlow's movements, but she hesitated about how much information to share. Despite Peter Jenson's assurances, Rachel had a nagging doubt.

"You'll be pleased to know we believe we've found the vulnerability," said Rachel.

Tamara's eyes widened, a flash of excitement crossing her features before she controlled her expression. "Uh? That's amazing."

"I've spoken to Captain Jenson about it, and we

would rather nobody else knows. Few people are aware there was a vulnerability in the first place. We're trusting you with this."

Rachel hesitated before reaching into her pocket. The weight of the micro-SD card felt disproportionately heavy for something so small. She handed it to Tamara. Peter had insisted she do so, despite her misgivings. Of course, she had a copy locked away in a drawer in her office – a precaution. If she was going to survive in this job, she had to create her own safety nets.

"It's supposedly on there. Captain Jenson would like you to examine it, and if you agree, he'll inform the relevant authorities."

Tamara's eyes narrowed, flicking from the card to Rachel's face. "I was beginning to think you didn't trust me," she said, an edge in her voice.

Rachel met her gaze. "Trust is earned in matters like this, and you've done just fine."

The tension between them crackled in the air for a moment. Rachel was following orders because Tamara had high clearance levels, and she and Peter weren't sure whether Bert Holland was involved yet. This was a calculated risk under difficult circumstances. "It's been a tricky situation over the past few days," said Rachel. "I'm sorry if it came across that way, but I had to be careful."

Tamara scrutinised the card, as though hypnotised by it, then she shrugged. "No, I get it, boss. I'd have done the same thing in your position. Although I'm sure the captain told you what I was doing here." Tamara grinned, the expression not quite reaching her eyes.

Rachel suppressed her unease. "Let's just put your skills to good use. You're on the vulnerability part of the investigation. The rest of the team will be on normal security and minor crimes, and a few of us are going to catch a killer. Please don't blur the boundaries."

Tamara leaned back in her chair, her posture relaxed, but her eyes alert. "That sounds good to me, boss. Catching killers isn't really what I'm good at." She paused, her smile widening. "Killing people, now that's another thing." Tamara laughed, the sound hollow.

Rachel didn't join in the laughter. "We each have our own skill set," she said, keeping her voice level. "Dedicate your time to this one. If there's something that can't wait, please contact me." Rachel turned to leave, but then looked back at Tamara. "If you're absolutely certain this is what we think it is, take it directly to Captain Jenson."

"Thanks for trusting me." Her emphasis on the word 'trusting' felt pointed. "I'll get on it straight away."

"Probably best if you don't do it here," said Rachel, glancing at the monitors.

Tamara raised an eyebrow. "Is there something else I should know?"

"Just that we need to keep this between a few of us,"

said Rachel. "And I don't want to take any chances. You can work in my office."

"Really?" Surprise flicked across the other woman's face.

"You'll have access to everything you need in there and won't be distracted by CCTV." Rachel didn't mention the hidden camera she'd installed. "Ravanos should relieve you in the next half hour."

"Okay, as soon as he's here, I'll go to your office. How do I get in?"

Rachel reached into her pocket and extracted a spare pass. Her fingers tightened around it before she handed it over. "This has a one-time code. It will get you in, but whatever you do, don't leave, because once the door self-locks, the code won't work again. Considering what happened the other night, it's so I can keep a check on who goes in and out."

Tamara took the pass, examining it with professional interest. "Good thinking," she said, sitting back down. Her smile returned, more genuine this time. "I'm glad we're on the same page now, boss."

Not quite, but close, thought Rachel, who wasn't as convinced as Peter was about giving an outsider so much access. The woman was clearly competent – perhaps too competent. Rachel had met enough military personnel to recognise the signs: careful control of facial expressions. Carlos and Jason both exhibited such signs when they needed to.

At least Rachel would know where her cyber expert would be over the next few hours.

Rachel didn't really want anything to do with this side of things. She couldn't claim to understand that what was on the memory card was what Carmen said it was and could understand Peter's reluctance to send it to the head office without some form of verification other than that of a retired spy.

If it turned out to be the vulnerability, it could be fixed. But if it wasn't, they needed to know. "I'll leave you to it," said Rachel, forcing a smile.

"I'll stay on the CCTV until Ravanos arrives. See you later, boss." Tamara's attention shifted back to the monitors, attempting to look relaxed, but she was a coiled spring.

Rachel could tell Tamara was itching to check the disk but had to trust she would follow her order. As she turned to leave, she glanced back at the person they were entrusting with sensitive information. She hoped Tamara's eagerness was conscientious rather than malicious. Captain Jenson trusted Tamara Shutt, but Rachel had learned the hard way that trust could be misplaced. People could wear many faces and play many roles. Those were the people who were the most dangerous.

Rachel stepped into the corridor, closing the door behind her. She leaned against the wall for a moment, taking a deep breath to steady herself. She had other things to do, other leads to follow.

The killer was still out there.

She radioed Peter and told him the disk was delivered and that Shutt was working in her office. As she headed away, she was reassured that her camera would watch Tamara the whole time she was in her office.

28

Rosemary Inglis shifted her weight from one foot to the other as she leaned against a wall at the back of one of the ship's galleys. All three of Belinda Marlow's auction winners were wide-eyed, bustling around a gleaming stainless-steel counter. Rosemary's assignment was to supervise the celebrity chef and look out for Sam Akbar.

Tantalising aromas of sautéed garlic and the delicate perfume of saffron wafted her way. The kitchen was a marvel in itself, with industrial-grade equipment. Stainless steel pans of every size hung in neat rows above a central island. Six professional-grade gas ranges lined one wall, while the opposite side featured huge refrigerators containing every ingredient necessary for the day's menus.

When Rosemary had first entered, introducing

herself and explaining that a member of the security team needed to be present because of the knives and other sharp objects, Belinda's smile had faltered.

Belinda soon forgot about Rosemary's presence as she joked and gestured while teaching the three winners how to cook one of her speciality dishes. The three winners, two middle-aged women and a slender older man, listened to every word. They were cooking one of the extravagant dishes from the menu the night before: pan-seared halibut with saffron risotto and lemon caper sauce. As a foodie herself, Rosemary was delighted with her duty.

"If you start with the saffron risotto," Belinda explained, "heat the olive oil in a saucepan over a medium heat. Make sure you don't use too high a temperature..."

Rosemary observed the three contenders following every instruction with varying degrees of skill, their faces a mixture of concentration and joy.

The older man, Charles, had his gas burner set too high, and smoke curled from his pan. Rosemary eyed the fire blanket, but Belinda got there first.

"Whoops, watch it there," she said, removing the pan from the heat. "I was only joking when I said 'burnt' was a new flavour last night."

Rosemary couldn't help grinning at the chef, who seemed very amicable as she reached for another pan, added oil, and then assisted Charles with the temperature.

"Now add the chopped garlic and the onion and sauté them until they are translucent," Belinda demonstrated, using her own pan. With a flick of the wrist, she sent the ingredients dancing across it. "After that, you're going to add arborio rice."

Rosemary forced herself to zone out while Belinda continued her cookery lesson. She was supposed to be watching what the chef did outside of the lesson – security, not cuisine.

A metal case sat near the door where Belinda's PA had placed it earlier. Unfortunately, Belinda hadn't opened it, apart from eyeing it several times, making Rosemary all the more intrigued to know what was inside. Each time Belinda's eyes drifted to it, a slight tension appeared around her mouth before she refocused on her students.

The three auction winners were enjoying themselves; two were more serious than the other. One woman moved with confident precision, while the other seemed more hesitant and starstruck. Charles's enthusiasm made up for his lack of skill.

"The secret to a perfect risotto," Belinda said, "is patience. You can't rush it." She demonstrated the slow addition of warm stock, ladling it into her rice mixture while stirring in rhythmic circles with a wooden spoon.

"Coax the starch out of the rice gently, like coaxing a secret from a friend."

Rosemary caught movement at the periphery of her vision. Someone was hovering near the doorway. She stepped sideways, positioning herself behind a tall shelving unit stocked with spices and dried goods. Through the gap, she could see Clint Foster talking to someone in the corridor lined with recycling bins just beyond the galley.

Belinda and her students were thoroughly engrossed in the cooking, the sizzle and steam creating a bubble of concentration around them. Rosemary sidled closer to the gap, grateful for the shelving's cover. At five-foot-ten with shoulders like a rugby prop, it was difficult to hide without knocking something over. Being muscular had its advantages, but it also had its disadvantages. Still, she was tall enough to peek over the shelving unit without being obvious.

Her muscles tensed. Clint was talking to the very person whom Rachel had asked her to keep a lookout for: Sam Akbar.

"She didn't show, I'm telling you," Rosemary heard Clint say, his voice low but carrying in the relative quiet of the corridor.

"So where is she?" Akbar asked, his posture tense. "You're supposed to be security, damn it."

Clint frowned, his jowls wobbling beneath his jaw

like unset gelatine. "I don't know, and I can't find out. The new chief of security's a control freak."

More like she's got you on a tight leash, thought Rosemary, her lips pressing together to suppress a smile. Rachel had briefed her thoroughly on the day's events, and Clint's unauthorised absence hadn't gone unnoticed.

"It's difficult to find out much information," Clint continued. "I took a tremendous risk getting to your restaurant. If she finds out, I'm in trouble."

You already are, Rosemary thought, shifting her weight to ease the tension in her right leg without making a noise.

"Why won't they tell you what's going on? You're supposed to keep a low profile," Akbar said, his voice rising before he checked himself.

"Look, I do keep a low profile, okay? But this new chief is difficult. She's picky and has formed a clique around her. The rest of us don't get a look-in, particularly those of us with more experience than her. Professional jealousy, I think they call it."

Rosemary bit the inside of her cheek. Rachel had inherited some longstanding members in her security team who were complacent and cut corners. If enforcing proper protocols made her part of a clique, then Rosemary was proud to be in it.

"Yeah, well, we don't have time for that," Akbar said,

glancing around. Rosemary picked up fear in his eyes. "You need to find Eleanor."

"If I'm going to put myself at risk, it's going to cost you more."

The crash of metal on tile cut through their conversation. Charles had dropped a pan, sending risotto splattering across the immaculate floor. The two men in the corridor jumped at the sound.

"I'll speak to Belinda later," Akbar said before moving out of earshot. They continued their conversation until they were out of sight. Rosemary couldn't hear what the rest of the conversation entailed.

Rosemary exhaled a slow breath. What was Sam Akbar even doing here, and what did he have to do with Belinda Marlow? At least it was clear Rachel's instincts had been right. It was Sam Akbar Eleanor was supposed to be meeting for lunch. But why hadn't he shown up? Why send Clint in his place?

Rosemary took a few steps back from her hiding spot and refocused her attention on the cooking class. Belinda was already turning chaos into calm while a kitchen porter cleared up the mess Charles had made.

"It's okay. We'll just start again from the beginning," Belinda reassured Charles, whose face had flushed a deep crimson. "You two carry on with what you're doing while I help Charles."

With practised efficiency, Belinda pulled together a

new set of ingredients, and Charles had a new risotto underway, his confidence bolstered by her patience.

The kitchen doors swung open, and Belinda's PA, dressed in a crisp trouser suit, entered, carrying a tablet close to her chest.

"How are we doing in here?" she asked, her eyes sweeping the kitchen.

"We're doing fine, Gill. How long have we got?" Belinda asked, briefly touching Charles's shoulder before stepping away to speak to her PA.

"Chef Mason says to give you a forty-minute warning, and then he'll need the kitchen to prepare the officers' dinners."

Belinda looked at the clock on the wall. "That's fine; we'll be finished in twenty."

Rosemary made a mental note to tell Rachel how Gill walked straight into the kitchen with no security check. Another breach of protocol.

The rest of the cookery lesson went well, with Belinda – despite her earlier lecture on patience when cooking risotto – performing the culinary equivalent of speed dating to get Charles caught up with his fellow winners. Soon, all three had produced relatively successful variations of the special dish.

"Beautiful!" Belinda exclaimed as she examined each. "These are exceptional first attempts."

The auction winners beamed under her praise and

sampled their creations, exclaiming over the flavours while Belinda offered a few final tips.

Once the students were dismissed, along with recipe cards and autographed aprons, Belinda cast a pointed glance toward Rosemary, her meaning clear: time for you to leave, too.

"I rarely have a security officer watching over me," she said, wiping down her station with efficient movements.

"The new chief of security is a stickler for the rules," said Rosemary, maintaining her position near the door. "Strictly speaking, you should have always had a member of our team with you."

"I suppose I'll have to get used to it," Belinda said, pursing her lips into a thin line. "But I'm used to coming and going as I like. I thought that had all been arranged."

"As I say," said Rosemary, crossing her arms over her chest, "there are no exceptions as far as Chief Jacobi-Prince is concerned. I'm just obeying orders." She softened her stance and relaxed her arms. "But I loved the class, by the way. Am I breaking confidentiality if I use that recipe at home?"

Belinda's expression thawed as she folded her knife roll. "No. That dish will be all over the internet by the time the cruise ends."

Rosemary watched, still wondering about the untouched metal case near the door. There was also something more to that knife roll. Belinda packed with unusual care. She picked up both the knife roll and the case, heading for the exit where Rosemary stood.

"I apologise, Ms Marlow, but you can't take those knives into the public areas of the ship."

Belinda's eyes widened. "What do you mean?"

"We can't have people walking around the ship with knives of any kind, especially not ones as well sharpened as those," said Rosemary, her tone apologetic but firm.

"This is too much, Officer Inglis," Belinda protested, her voice rising several decibels. "I've been walking around the ship with these knives ever since I arrived. Why is it suddenly an issue?"

"I'm sorry, but you should never have been allowed to keep a roll of knives with you." Rosemary stood her ground, her broader frame effectively blocking the doorway. "Previous oversights don't justify security risks."

"We'll see about this," Belinda said, drawing herself up to her full height, which still left her several inches shorter than Rosemary. "I'll speak to Captain Jenson. What's the name of your new chief again? Perhaps I'd better have a word with her."

"Rachel Jacobi-Prince, ma'am." Rosemary remained in position, unmoved by the threat to go over her head. "In the meantime, I will need to take those."

"These are my special knives," Belinda said,

clutching the roll tighter. "I can't have anything happening to them. There's no way I'm just handing them over to you."

Rosemary considered the standoff, then offered a compromise. "Then let's find a middle ground. Come with me."

Belinda reluctantly followed Rosemary out of the kitchen and down a short corridor lined with storage lockers. She selected an unused one and opened it. "Please place the knife roll in there."

Belinda complied with a huff of frustration, carefully placing the roll inside the metal locker. Rosemary locked the door and handed Belinda the key.

"There you are. That's for you to keep until you disembark."

Belinda relaxed. "So, only I have access to that locker?"

"Yes," said Rosemary with a smile. "I'll also need to check the contents of the metal case before you leave," she added.

Belinda's scowl returned. "Is this really necessary?"

"The safety of our passengers is our top priority, so yes, I'm afraid so."

"It's got a few things inside you might deem unsafe. Perhaps I'll put it in the locker with the knife roll."

Rosemary watched as Belinda opened the locker and added the small case before locking it again. What she didn't tell the chef was that Rachel had master keys for each of them.

Belinda turned to face Rosemary. "Satisfied, Officer Inglis?"

"Thank you for your co-operation," said Rosemary with a nod. She gestured for Belinda to accompany her back to the public areas of the ship. "Would you like me to ask the chief of security to meet you?"

"No need. I'll deal with it. Thank you." Belinda was about to march off but must have reconsidered. She spun around with a forced smile. "Nice to meet you, Officer Inglis, and I'm so pleased you enjoyed my cookery lesson. Please feel free to come again."

Trust me, I will, thought Rosemary, saying, "Thank you. Enjoy your evening."

As soon as Belinda was out of sight, Rosemary checked her watch. Almost time for her meeting with Rachel. She headed to the Jazz Bar, where Rachel had asked her and Jason to meet while Tamara was using Rachel's office. Her mind raced with questions. Most intriguing of all – what was in the metal case Belinda had been so reluctant to open? She had a lot to report.

29

Rachel rapped on the door of the stateroom suite, with Rosemary by her side. Rosemary had told her about her observations when they'd met with Jason the evening before. The ship had left Nuuk at midnight, arriving at Amerloq Fjord in the early hours. Although the ship had dropped anchor, passengers weren't being cleared to leave yet.

The man opened the door, his eyes wide when he saw them.

"Mr Akbar, my name is Rachel Jacobi-Prince. I'm the chief of security, and this is Rosemary Inglis, one of our security officers. May we come in and have a word?"

"If you wish." Akbar stood to one side, allowing Rachel to pass, but Rosemary waited for him to follow Rachel so that she could bring up the rear.

"What is this about, Chief?"

Chapter 29

Sam Akbar was playing it cool. "For a dead man, you're looking remarkably well," Rachel said.

Surprised, he hesitated before regaining his composure. "I'm not sure I follow."

"It's just that you have a remarkable way of disappearing and reappearing without a trace," said Rosemary. "We understand you boarded the *Meridian Queen* for its maiden voyage and were presumed to have gone overboard. And yet, here you are."

"That was a misunderstanding."

"Perhaps you could explain how you survived such a fall," said Rachel.

"I didn't fall. Your crew got it wrong."

"In which case, you might like to explain how you disembarked the ship in New York with no record of you doing so."

Sam Akbar flopped into a chair. "Perhaps you would like to take a seat," he said.

Rachel sat while Rosemary remained standing, ready for any unexpected movements.

Akbar cleared his throat. "I'm afraid it's a matter of state security, Chief. I'm sure you'll understand."

"While in Greenland, we come under Danish law, and you have no immunity. Whatever games you've played in the past, Mr Akbar, I will not allow you to spy on board this ship. Please, could you tell me what you're doing on board the *Coral Queen*?"

"Taking a cruise; what else would I be doing?"

"Mr Akbar, I haven't got time for this. I know you were in a relationship with Eleanor Brodie." The tremor in his hand told Rachel she was on the right track.

"Have you arrested her? She has done nothing wrong."

"I'm afraid it's far more serious than that, Mr Akbar," said Rosemary. "Eleanor Brodie's body was discovered in the ship's laundry two nights ago."

Akbar dropped all sense of control, leaning forward with his head in his hands. "My God. What happened?"

"We were hoping you'd be able to help with that," said Rachel. "You were meant to meet for lunch yesterday and sent someone in your place. What I wish to know is whether that was an act to convince people you didn't kill her or whether you had something to do with her death?"

Sam Akbar remained in stunned silence, but his eyes met hers. She continued.

"As you have the ability to play Houdini, we need to talk about several things."

"Look, what I do is in the national interests of my country. I can't talk about that, but I can assure you that Eleanor and I were close."

"Even though she ended the relationship," said Rachel.

His eyes filled as they looked at her. "We loved each other. It's very difficult when you've got your country's national interests to take care of. After we got back together and made sure we didn't cross those lines, we met when we could. You're right; we were due to meet on this cruise."

"Why should we believe you? For all we know, you could be a double agent." Rachel would not be taken in by a professional liar.

"I'm not a double agent."

"So why the Houdini act? Was that another misunderstanding?" said Rosemary, a cynical edge to her voice.

"I was being watched. That's why I had to disappear. As soon as I could, I let Eleanor know I was alive. She had ended our relationship, but I'm telling you, we got back together. When she didn't turn up at dinner the other night, I was worried. We were supposed to meet for lunch in Nuuk, but I couldn't risk walking into a trap. I didn't know if she'd reconsidered and was going to keep what she'd found to herself."

"We don't believe Eleanor was working for British Intelligence," said Rosemary.

"Of course she was."

"She may have gone freelance, so anything you shared with her could have been sold to the highest bidder. I'm afraid you've been outmanoeuvred."

Akbar was shocked. His shoulders heaved before switching from grief to anger.

"She would never do that."

"Did you kill her, Mr Akbar?"

"No, of course not. I've just told you I loved her."

"And yet you didn't turn up for lunch yesterday as arranged."

"I already told you, I didn't turn up because I didn't know what was going on. I sent someone else."

"Ah. Yes, Clint Foster; I wondered when we might get around to him. A member of my security team. It appears you have a way of dragging people into your treachery," said Rachel, still seething about the Foster situation, especially after being informed by Rosemary about the clandestine meeting with Akbar. "How did you get him to work for you?"

"Okay, Chief, you've got me. Clint was easy to manipulate, and his motive – good old-fashioned money. He's not your number one fan, by the way."

"That works both ways," said Rachel. "But he won't be working for this cruise line, or any other, for much longer, so I suggest you find another lackey. And unfortunately, Mr Akbar, I will not allow you to leave the ship today."

"But I have important meetings."

"Consider them cancelled until further notice," said Rachel.

"You can't do this. I have diplomatic immunity."

"Then report me. Oh no, you can't because while you're on board this ship, I can do whatever I want with you," said Rachel. "You are under house arrest, but if you'd like me to make it more uncomfortable, I could put you in the brig."

He held his hands, palms in the air, a gesture of surrender. "Okay, okay, but I'm telling you, I had nothing to do with Eleanor's death. Why would I kill her? We had worked things out."

"The problem with bribery and corruption," said Rachel, "is you never know who works for whom, do you? I wonder if she was going to sell you out."

Akbar shook his head. "There was no reason to. I wasn't a risk to her; we were on the same side. Mostly."

"You still haven't said what you're doing on board the *Coral Queen*. Tell me that, and I might listen."

"The truth is, I came to see Eleanor, but I was aware of an IT issue. We shared the same goal there."

Rachel glared at him. "From what I hear, Eleanor wasn't the sharing kind. Maybe your mission was more important than your so-called love."

"I work for the United States, but I can't share any more than that. Do your worst. I'll be free in no time. In fact, you probably need to lock me up because if I find who murdered Eleanor, I will kill them."

"What is your relationship to Belinda Marlow?" Rachel asked.

"You really have been busy," said Sam. "Belinda loves being a celebrity, and she also likes the good life. Americans pay well."

Rachel's eyebrow shot up, her head spinning. "Pay well for what?"

"Look, it's difficult to transport surveillance equipment sometimes, particularly on cruise ships. Being a social media celebrity, Belinda's allowed to bring on board a lot of recording stuff. She gets paid for transportation."

"And why did you want to speak to her yesterday evening?" Rachel asked.

"When? Oh, you were watching Clint, I suppose. I don't blame you. I wouldn't trust him either."

"And yet you sent him on a lunch errand," said Rosemary. "I overheard the two of you speaking outside the galley yesterday."

"I had to find out whether Eleanor had changed her mind about seeing me." He returned his attention to Rachel. "Belinda's been carrying equipment for me and I needed something for today. I think she also secretly films your chefs' preparations for new material. As long as she moves things for me, I don't mind if she uses it from time to time."

Rachel knew about the galley filming, having received information from Rosemary that they had looked inside the locker Belinda was using and found the equipment Sam mentioned. Perhaps he was telling the truth after all.

"You realise we'll need to verify what you've said with Ms Marlow?"

Doubt appeared in Sam's eyes. "You can try, but I don't think she'll own up to working for the Americans. You might find the other stuff, though. I can give you a list of our equipment if it helps."

"We've already discovered what she was up to, so we will take that line of questioning. Please don't test my resolve, Mr Akbar. Stay in your stateroom. I'll leave an officer outside."

"Won't that draw attention to me?"

"Would you prefer the brig?"

"In this instance, I might," he said with a charming smile. Rachel could see why Eleanor fell for him.

Rachel gave Rosemary a nod. "Please lock your mobile phone and any other devices in your safe unless you would like us to store them for you."

"No need. I'll put them in the safe."

Rachel left Rosemary to deal with Sam Akbar while she met Jason in her office. How did these people weave so many lies? And how was she going to hunt down Eleanor's killer when she was overwhelmed by subterfuge?

30

Clint was waiting outside Rachel's office when she arrived. His face was like thunder.

"I'll be with you in a minute," she said, unlocking the door and going inside to answer the desk phone. "Hello, Chief of Security here?"

"Rachel, it's Peter. I just wanted to give you an update on the vulnerability you found."

By accident, thought Rachel. Tamara had left a note on her desk the night before to say it was what they were looking for, and she'd taken it to Captain Jenson. "Is it fixed?"

"Head office is working on it. The awkward thing is that they had inside help, as you suspected. It appears the late Ms Brodie was meeting someone that night."

Rachel held her breath. "Who?"

"Tamara did a great job finding it, as the details were well hidden."

Right now, all Rachel wanted was a name. She would give Tamara due praise later. "Was it someone from IT?"

"You're ahead of me again," he said. "I suppose you know who it was?" There was a lightness in Peter's voice, and she couldn't blame him for that. They had found something that would have put the entire fleet at risk were it not for Eleanor Brodie's diligence and determination. But Rachel still had a killer to find. "I'm guessing Bert Holland."

She heard the audible sigh at the other end of the phone and knew she was right. Graham Bentley had discovered that Bert's wife had died under suspicious circumstances, which the Swiss police were investigating, but Bert was insisting it was a genuine mistake and was asking the police to drop the case. "That's the other reason for calling," Peter's voice had switched to being flat. "Can you speak to him? I don't have the heart. I've worked with Bert for over ten years. I never believed he would be involved in something like this."

"Where is he now?" Rachel asked.

"In my quarters. I've asked him to stay there until you arrive."

"Has he admitted to the murder?"

"He won't speak. I think he's scared."

"Okay. I've just got someone else to interview, and then I'll be up," said Rachel. Did they have their killer at last? She replaced the handset in its receiver and looked up as Jason entered. Concern filled his eyes.

"Is something the matter?"

"The vulnerability has been confirmed and is being sorted, but the bad news is Bert Holland was the person Eleanor was meeting with."

Jason's expression said it all. Too much treachery from people they trusted. "Was it blackmail, or was he selling us out as well?"

"We'll find out soon enough. Let's deal with him first." Rachel motioned to the door.

Jason turned and called Clint Foster inside. He scowled at Jason on his way past, lumbering to the chair opposite her desk, which once again creaked under his heavy frame.

"What's this about? I have work to do." His voice was almost a snarl.

"It's time we had another chat," said Rachel, pleased that this time Jason was with her. He pulled up a chair, deliberately placing it next to Clint. She looked up to see Ravanos at the door. All bases covered if he kicked off.

"What about now?"

"Let's begin with your dereliction of duty. You left your post yesterday."

"I had personal matters to deal with."

"And there was I thinking you were drinking at the Hotel Hans Egede."

"Whoever told you that is lying. I had an emergency."

"I saw you there."

A flash of fear crossed Clint's face before it turned to anger. "You have no right to spy on me."

"Why don't you tell me about your work for Sam Akbar?"

"I don't know what you're talking about." He turned to Jason. "You're not going to sit there and let her talk to me like this, are you? Waverley would never have made false accusations."

"Chief Waverley," Jason corrected, a flintlike look in his eyes.

Rachel continued. "Mr Akbar's already confirmed that you were at the hotel at his request. Even if he hadn't, you were overheard discussing a passenger named Eleanor Brodie with him." Rachel observed his reaction. He was shifting in his chair as he had during their previous meeting. "I'm also assuming it was you who allowed him to disembark the *Meridian Queen* when he was reported to have gone overboard. I've checked the records and know you were filling in at that time while they expanded the security team on the new ship. Convenient."

Clint folded his arms in disgust. "You have nothing on me."

"Seriously?" Jason snapped.

"I've got plenty on you. Sam Akbar says you are on his payroll, and Officer Inglis overheard your conversation with Mr Akbar yesterday. If you think he's going to protect you, I suggest you think again."

"I needed the money, all right?"

"What did you need the money for?" Rachel asked.

"I'm saving to get out of this life. Buy myself a piece of real estate and do what the hell I like."

"Alas," said Rachel, "the money train is about to leave the station. I don't know how many regulations you've broken, or whether there will be any charges, but I can confirm that you no longer work for Queen Cruises. You are fired with immediate effect."

"Why?"

Jason exhaled. "If you had any sense of decency, you wouldn't need to ask that question."

"There's a more serious matter I need to speak to you about," said Rachel. "Did you have anything to do with Eleanor Brodie's murder?"

Clint dropped all aggression, staring at her with wide eyes. His mouth dropped open. He was genuinely shocked.

"Eleanor's dead? Does Sam know?"

"Yes, he does. And we need to find her killer. What can you tell me?"

Clint shook his head. "I didn't know. All I did was

break a few rules here and there. You can't pin murder on me."

Rachel was satisfied. "Ravanos will escort you to the brig, and I'll discuss your case with Captain Jenson. At the very least, we'll drop you off in New York."

"You can't do that to me."

"I can and I will," said Rachel. "Consider your days as an employee of this cruise line over. It's a shame you couldn't just do your job. My discussion with Captain Jenson will be about whether we charge you, which also depends on what else we find. Allowing people like Sam Akbar and Belinda Marlow access to restricted parts of our ship may have put lives at risk, and considering what Belinda was up to with her surveillance equipment, could have led to industrial espionage."

Clint glared at Rachel, who gave the nod to Ravanos.

Rachel held out her hand. "Your pass, please."

Ravanos escorted Clint from the room. "Should I go with him?" Jason asked.

"No. He's a playground bully. I don't think he'll give us any more trouble. I don't think he understands just how stupid he's been."

"That's the trouble with men like that," said Jason. "Give them a bit of power and they abuse it. I don't think he killed Eleanor, though."

Rachel exhaled. "Me neither. Time to speak to Bert."

31

Rachel briefed Peter Jenson on the situations involving Clint Foster and Sam Akbar. "Sometimes I don't believe I know what's going on aboard this ship at all," he said.

"Nobody can stop spies from doing what they do," said Rachel. "Thanks to Eleanor, we've prevented cyber terrorists or hackers associated with cyber criminals from doing us great harm."

"You're right. Ignore me." Peter seemed tired. It had been a tough few days for all of them. "I'll take you through to Bert."

Peter left Rachel and Jason with Bert Holland, who looked broken. Rachel was in no doubt: Bert had somehow been forced into the predicament he was now in, but if he had killed Eleanor, justice must be served.

"Can you tell me why you were meeting Eleanor Brodie on Sunday night?" she asked.

Bert looked down at his trembling hands, saying nothing.

"Did you kill her?"

Bert's head shot up, terror in his eyes as if about to say something, but then his shoulders sagged, and he clammed up.

"It would help if you told us why you put the fleet at risk," said Jason.

Bert shook his head. "That's not what happened."

"So what did happen?" Rachel asked gently. "You have a perfect record. I don't believe you would have betrayed us for no reason."

"This woman approached me in Barcelona... I was on shore leave... she knew everything about me... about my wife... she asked me to help her..." Tears welled in his eyes as he looked around the room. "...to find something in our systems. She said people wanted to sell it."

"Can I just clarify you're talking about Eleanor Brodie?" Rachel asked.

Bert nodded, tears now falling freely down his face. "I wasn't sure at first, but she said it was of the utmost importance and that I would be doing the cruise line a huge favour."

"Why didn't she approach the cruise line with this information?" Jason asked.

"Because she thought that by the time it went through all the official channels, the vulnerability would be stolen and sold. Major hacks are big money these days. She then..." His shoulders heaved as he sobbed out his grief, sniffing before starting again. "... Eleanor knew my wife was dying."

Graham had discovered that Bert's wife had terminal cancer and wasn't having minor surgery as they had thought. Although there had been a drug error, her time was limited to months rather than years. "Why did you say it was minor surgery?"

"In terms of her cancer, it was. The doctors were creating a bypass in her bile duct to provide palliative symptom relief. The thing is that my wife had had enough. She wanted to die."

"And the drug error prevented her from getting euthanasia?" Jason asked.

"No. She couldn't go for euthanasia. The kids would never forgive us if she did. But she wanted to die."

Rachel was forming a picture in her head. "You asked Eleanor to help?"

Bert swallowed hard, tears drying up. "My wife was desperate, and there was no other way. Eleanor told me, as a gesture of goodwill, she could help, but that we had to move fast. I took a day's leave and flew to see my wife and explained that I knew someone who could give her the death she wanted. I asked her to consider whether it was what she really wanted and told her I wouldn't be able to be there."

He wiped a few more tears roughly from his face before looking at them both. "She was in terrible pain – hiding it from the kids all the time was unbearable. We said our goodbyes, and I came back to the ship."

Rachel recalled how Bernard had told Sarah that Bert was not the same man he had been. The guilt must have been killing him, let alone the pressure Eleanor was putting him under.

"And Eleanor kept her promise."

He nodded. "She arranged for someone – I don't know how – to give her the wrong dose."

Jason's face tensed, no doubt imagining Sarah being put in such a horrible position. "What happened to the nurse?" he asked.

"I wasn't told. They said it might have been an agency nurse who gave the injection and were unsure about it. I told them not to pursue it, that mistakes happen, because I would have felt even more guilty if anyone got into trouble over it. It only came to me recently that Eleanor might have sent someone to the hospital dressed as a nurse to give her the lethal injection."

Eleanor Brodie's modus operandi. Rachel tried to suppress her anger. "It explains why you only took a few weeks' compassionate leave. What happened with Eleanor?"

"We met in Reykjavik, and she told me what to look for. I found what I thought it was and copied it to the encrypted micro-SD card she had given me. When I gave it to her, she warned me to be careful. She seemed frightened and said there could be an assassin on board."

"I don't suppose she gave a name?" Jason asked, folding his arms.

"No. She took the card, said she would need to check it, and we were meant to meet in the laundry at 1 a.m. in case she needed me to do anything else. When the storm hit and the blackout occurred, I couldn't meet her. The next thing I heard, she had died."

"Could she have caused the blackout?"

"After she died, I panicked and checked for other anomalies. Something in the code triggered the blackout. It had to be someone on board, so yes, it could have been her."

"Or the assassin," said Rachel, feeling more frustrated than ever. "Could another person have jammed our CCTV monitoring system?"

"If they hacked the system, yes. The vulnerability was harder to find, but a good hacker could cause camera glitches, especially during a storm when the systems would be under pressure."

"So we're no nearer to finding our killer," said Jason, sounding as frustrated as Rachel was feeling.

"You need to tell Peter everything you've told us,"

said Rachel. "You should have come to me instead of working for an outside source."

"I would have told Peter if it wasn't for the situation with my wife."

Rachel gave Jason a nod and suggested they leave. On the way out, she gave a brief summary to Peter and told him Bert would fill in the details. When they left the bridge, she squeezed Jason's arm. "Don't judge him too harshly. I don't condone euthanasia, especially not illegally, like in this case, but many do. He was stuck between two evils."

"It's not so much that, but an innocent nurse has most likely taken the blame."

Rachel was already considering that and believed Eleanor would have used an outside source. Even she wouldn't have let a genuine nurse take the blame. "The important thing now is that he's not our killer. We know where he was when Eleanor died, and if Sam and Clint are telling the truth, it has to be someone else."

"Belinda Marlow?"

"Maybe. There's also Tamara Shutt, who's well capable of hacking into our systems." And somebody else sprang to Rachel's mind. "We need to move."

32

Sarah had just finished morning surgery and was heading off to meet Jason for lunch before they left for an afternoon of shore leave.

She noticed the older woman, Charlotte Kieft, in the main atrium. Sarah hadn't been formally introduced but could see that Charlotte seemed preoccupied, watching someone.

"Good morning," Sarah said to Charlotte but got no reply. Following Charlotte's line of sight, she saw Alex Reyes. "Oh, hello, Alex. How are you?"

"I'm good, thanks." He smiled, but it seemed forced. "Sorry about the misunderstanding the other day."

"No problem. I'm as good as new. Are you going ashore?"

"Yeah, free at last. I can't wait to get my feet on land."

Chapter 32

Charlotte Kieft was staring at both of them through narrowed eyes.

Sarah wasn't sure what to make of Rachel's new friend, who appeared very tense. Alex seemed happy; he'd obviously recovered from the trauma of losing his boss. From what Jason had told her, Rachel was about to arrest someone for Eleanor's murder, so she was filled with excited anticipation. "Enjoy your day," she said to Alex.

"Thanks, I will," he replied.

Sarah turned to speak to Charlotte, but she was hurrying off the ship. She shrugged and headed to Rachel's office to find Jason. "Good to see you both. I hear you're making progress," she said.

"Yes and no," Rachel replied. "We're following leads and uncovering most of the crimes, but still don't have the murderer. Clint Foster handled Sam Akbar and Belinda Marlow's clandestine activities. Sam Akbar works for the Americans, and Belinda was helping him. We believe he was looking for the same thing as Eleanor, but if he's to be believed, they were still an item. Clint's whereabouts for the night of the storm have been confirmed. He had drunk too much and had to be helped to bed by a couple of crewmen."

Jason added, "Bert Holland was the one who found the vulnerability and gave it to Eleanor. He was the person she was supposed to meet in the laundry but couldn't because of the chaos."

Sarah felt her jaw drop. "Long story," Rachel said. "Sam sent Clint on his lunch errand, suspecting something was going on when Eleanor wasn't at the VIP dinner. He thought she had shut him out of the investigation."

"That explains why Clint turned up for lunch. And what about the disk Carmen checked for you?"

"Verified," Rachel said. "It's being fixed as we speak."

"It's very confusing. Is one of them lying then?" Sarah asked.

"Maybe," Rachel replied. She had that thoughtful look on her face that told Sarah she was putting the pieces together. Having known her since childhood, Sarah could read the signs.

"My money's on Foster," said Jason.

"Whether or not your money's on Foster, you and I are going out for the afternoon. I've enjoyed being back at work, but now I'd like to tour a little piece of Greenland with my husband." Jason was hesitant, so Sarah looked at Rachel. "Is he free, Rachel?"

"Yes, of course. You two go out. I need time to think through this nonsense."

"I just saw your new friend Charlotte in the main atrium," said Sarah.

"How was she?"

"Distracted, I'd say. She seemed to be watching Alex, but maybe she was waiting to get onto a tender."

"Alex Reyes?" Rachel asked, suddenly stiffening.

"Yes, he looked well. He was looking forward to getting ashore, he said."

"What do you mean?" Rachel asked.

Sarah looked at her friend and realised that something was amiss. "He was boarding a tender to go out for the day."

"No way," said Rachel, getting onto the radio. "Ravanos. Get up to Alex Reyes' room now and check on our security officer."

Moments later, the radio buzzed into life. "Tied up, boss. Reyes has made a run for it."

"Ravanos, get down to that tunnel that leads from the laundry to the MI and check it with a fine toothcomb. You're looking for blood where someone gashed their arm."

Sarah realised immediately what Rachel was referring to: the mystery gash on Alex Reyes' arm.

"I'm so sorry," said Rachel, looking at Sarah but already heading for the door, followed by Jason. "I need your husband."

Sarah felt her heart race. "I understand. Go get him."

33

Alex Reyes had already passed through security and gone ashore.

By the time Rachel and Jason arrived in their own tender, weaving through passengers eager to explore the Greenlandic fjord, he was nowhere in sight. The streets were filled with tourists and vendors selling handcrafted art.

"Okay, we need to contact the local police," Rachel said, scanning the bustling crowd.

Jason looked in every direction. "Where will he be heading?" he asked, his voice urgent.

"I can't believe I've been so duped," said Rachel, adjusting her jacket, the only thing she'd had time to collect in their hurry to leave the ship. Neither of them was dressed for the weather.

"He's clever," said Jason. "That's why he managed the frightened, innocent act that had us all convinced."

"He's gone to the northern end of the fjord."

Rachel turned at the sound of the voice to see Charlotte Kieft at the back of a tour group. She was dressed for the weather; a thick woollen coat and knee-length fur-lined suede boots shielding her from the cold and the wind. She looked every bit as knowledgeable as when Rachel first met her.

"Who are you referring to?" Rachel moved closer, not quite believing their luck.

"That good-looking young man who I saw Eleanor avoiding and who was in Eleanor's room this morning," Charlotte said matter-of-factly.

"Was he indeed?" said Rachel, exchanging a meaningful glance with Jason.

"He said he was a software engineer working with Eleanor. I don't know what he was looking for or how he got into her room, but his face told me he didn't find it. And I didn't believe him for a minute, which is why I followed him ashore. I heard him tell a taxi driver where he was going."

"Thanks for the information, Charlotte." I wish you'd come straight to me, she thought but said, "Enjoy your day."

"You too, Rachel," she said with a twinkle in her eye. "I hope you catch him." She tapped her embroidered bag. "I have pepper spray if you need it."

Rachel couldn't help chuckling. "Thanks, but we'll manage." Rachel and Jason climbed into a taxi, a weathered vehicle with extra heaters for which she was grateful. The driver nodded when she told him where to go and to be as quick as he could.

"I can get you there in twenty-five minutes." He pulled away from the kerb, manoeuvring through narrow streets with practiced ease.

"Why would Alex kill Eleanor?" Jason asked, turning his head to look at Rachel as he leaned back in his seat. "She employed him."

"I don't think she employed him at all," Rachel said, her mind racing as the last pieces of the puzzle fell into place. "We only have his word for that, and I believe he's been taking us for fools since the moment we caught him when Sarah was injured. The only truth he told us was that he's a hacker. I was thinking earlier about who the most likely suspect was after excluding most of the others. When Sarah first met Alex, he was close to the M1 corridor; no doubt, having realised he'd dropped the micro-SD card, he was retracing his steps."

"After gashing his arm."

"I believe so."

"But then he got injured again," said Jason, rubbing his chin.

Rachel glanced out of the window. The colourful houses were giving way to the sparser outskirts, smaller buildings dotting the rocky landscape against a backdrop of ice-capped mountains. "And more importantly, Sarah found him. She was lucky something else happened that made him run."

Jason's face paled, and his eyes filled with the anger she'd seen when they found Sarah injured in Alex's stateroom. His hands clenched into fists on his lap. "So, he wasn't checking her pulse. He was going to kill her."

Rachel hated to think how close Sarah had come to losing her life in the Coral Restaurant but didn't think Alex would have risked killing her in his room. She thanked God that her best friend was still alive. The taxi hit a pothole, jostling them. "He's the assassin Eleanor told Bert about, and that Charlotte noticed Eleanor avoiding." Noting Jason's confusion, she added, "Sorry, I forgot to mention that. Plus, he's a hacker, no doubt working for a criminal organisation. I think Eleanor orchestrated the blackout to test the vulnerability while the security camera glitches were most likely orchestrated by Alex while he waited for his prey."

"And the disconnecting of the cameras overlooking the M1 corridor?"

"Yes. I thought that was Clint, but as far as I can tell, he isn't in Alex's pocket," said Rachel. "Alex could have hacked into the ship's plans and worked out he might need an escape route. My bet is he wore a crew uniform to disconnect the cameras himself or it could have been Eleanor who did that; we know she was careful and had several uniforms to choose from."

"But how did Alex know about Eleanor and Bert's meeting?" Jason's brow furrowed.

"Who knows? He could have bugged her, or more likely Bert, once he realised who she was working with. Eleanor would be too clever to fall for it, but not Bert." Rachel looked out at the small farms coming into view.

"So, he let Eleanor check for the vulnerability and then waited for her in the laundry," said Jason. "We should have locked him up after he attacked Sarah."

Rachel didn't need reminding of that fact, but Sarah herself had told them he was about to let her go. Maybe he was checking for a pulse like he said, but he had still played them. "Eleanor took advantage of the storm to cause the blackout, and he took advantage of it to kill Eleanor and steal the memory card."

"But if he knew about the vulnerability, why did he need the memory card?" Jason asked, scratching his head while looking at the road ahead.

"He may have known about it but didn't have access to it, or he had to stop it from being found and reported so he could sell the information. I expect he was also after the agent dossier that Carmen held on to," Rachel replied, then leaned forward to speak to the driver. "Can you go any faster?"

The driver did as instructed, pressing down on the accelerator. The old taxi protested with a groan but picked up speed as it wound along the coastal road. Rachel could see a seaplane in the distance, perched near a flat plain, with the dramatic fjord and icebergs as a backdrop.

While the taxi bumped along, Rachel contacted the ship to tell the local police where they were headed. Rosemary promised to relay the message, but Rachel wasn't sure help would arrive in time.

They passed an empty taxi going in the opposite direction and soon after arrived at the rugged piece of land where it was possible to access the plane, Rachel told the driver to stop. She and Jason jumped out of the taxi. Rachel fumbled in her pockets for kroner and thrust them at the driver. "Please wait here."

The ground was rocky and fraught with danger. A small boat was waiting not far from the shore. Rachel saw Alex Reyes in the distance, clambering across rocks toward the waiting boat that would transport him to the seaplane.

"Quick," she yelled, pointing.

A gigantic man in dark sunglasses and a thick black fleece, tight across his muscular chest, stepped out from behind a hillock, barring their way. His stance was professional and menacing – private security no doubt.

"You deal with him; I'll deal with Reyes," said Rachel, not sure Jason could control himself if she let him loose on Alex. Not to mention the size of the beast blocking their way.

"Oh great," said Jason, his voice dripping with sarcasm. Then, with determination, he ran at the man like a rugby tackler and managed to wind him, knocking them both to the ground in a tangle of limbs.

Rachel clambered after Alex, who didn't hear her approach because of the sound of the motorboat revving up. The chill from the harsh grasses permeating the rocks and the cold from the fjord penetrated her shoes. The smell of jet fuel filled her nostrils. She managed to get close enough to Alex to reach for his arm, grateful that regular jogging meant she wasn't even breathless.

"Going somewhere, Alex?"

He spun around, eyes wide in shock, and dropped the briefcase he was carrying. It hit the rocks and tumbled down with a clatter. His face, which had seemed so fearful and trustworthy when they first met, was now twisted with rage.

"Chief," he said, his voice eerily calm. "You should have stayed on the ship and let me go. It's not like a chief of security should abandon her post."

"And it's not like a chief of security would let you get away with murder," Rachel replied, keeping her distance.

An evil smile crossed his face. "We do what we have to do."

"And all for money. Shame you didn't get what you wanted."

"There's always a next time," he said.

"Not if I have my way," she said.

Remembering this man could kill a woman with his bare hands, she was ready when he suddenly lunged. She sidestepped his attack, using her palm to slam into his nose, just as she had done when she first encountered him.

He yelled and staggered backwards, blood streaming from his nose, his eyes watering. "You'll regret that," he snarled.

Rachel circled cautiously, wishing she was wearing more appropriate footwear. She watched for an opening. "It's over, Alex. The police are on their way."

With surprising speed, he lunged at her again. This time, Rachel wasn't quite fast enough. His shoulder caught her in the stomach, forcing the air from her lungs. She stumbled backwards but stayed on her feet, gasping for breath.

Alex pressed his advantage, swinging a fist toward her face. Rachel ducked just in time, feeling the blast of air from his punch sail over her head and into the hill behind her. He cursed. She countered with a kick to his shin that made him howl and used a karate chop to send him tumbling to the floor. She managed to pin his arms behind his back and keep him on the ground.

He struggled and broke free from her grip, using his heightened state to escape. Before she could back away, he hit out at her with a wild swing. She felt the thump on her chin, which brought stars to her eyes. Rachel staggered, momentarily dazed. Alex moved in for another blow, but she dropped to one knee, causing his punch to miss. Then she surged upward, driving her shoulder into his midsection.

Alex grunted in pain and stumbled backwards down the incline, where he landed next to his briefcase. He fell hard onto the rocks, hitting the back of his head with an audible clunk. He lay still, unconscious but alive.

Jason, having finally subdued the security guard in what looked like a painful arm lock, called out to her. "Rachel! Are you okay?"

"I'm fine," she called, stroking her tender chin with one hand while picking up the briefcase with the other.

In the distance, Rachel could hear sirens approaching. The motorboat had joined the seaplane, and she watched the plane moving away. Alex groaned, trying to push himself up.

"Don't even think about it," she warned. "Anyway, it seems your ride got tired of waiting."

Alex stared at the plane as it took off, his face bloodied and eyes defeated.

As the local police cars screeched to a halt further up the hill, Rachel felt a wave of relief wash over her. She looked at Jason walking toward her, dragging the subdued security guard with him.

"We did it," she said, smiling despite her throbbing chin.

The crisp Greenlandic air whipped around them as

the police officers handcuffed Alex and the security guard. The briefcase contained Alex's laptop, which no doubt would reveal more evidence of what he was up to. She put gloves on and lifted two items from the case.

"The cloned key card," she said. "And Eleanor's phone." Rachel returned the items and handed the briefcase to one of the police officers with a satisfied smile.

Sometimes her new duties involved mundane tasks like lost passports and excessive drinking, but today she and Jason had fulfilled the most important part of the job: keeping people safe.

34

Rachel had heard that Tamara Shutt was leaving to return to her job, so she waited by the exit.

Tamara grinned as she approached in full military uniform. "Sorry I couldn't be honest with you," she said.

"I understand," replied Rachel. "Sorry I couldn't trust you."

Tamara shrugged. "We got there in the end."

I'm not sure we did, thought Rachel, but now wasn't the time. "Thanks for your help."

"Just doing my job."

"About your job," Rachel said, "why was British military intelligence interested in a cruise ship vulnerability?"

Tamara smiled. "Goodbye, Chief. It's been a pleasure."

"Goodbye, Tamara."

Chapter 34

Rachel watched her go, glad not to have to slink in the shadows of spiery as Sarah would put it.

∽

Over dinner in the officers' dining room that evening, Rachel and Jason received many congratulatory slaps on the back. Peter Jenson had been the first to thank them.

"What happens now?" Sarah asked, tucking into a well-deserved steak.

"Peter has informed MI6 that Alex Reyes murdered one of their officers – she was still working for them, by the way – and they'll deal with his extradition. That's out of our hands now, and the vulnerability has been fixed. Eleanor was assigned her mission when MI6 heard online chatter, and realised such a vulnerability would be of interest to cyber criminals and terrorists. Although the cruise line was aware of its existence, they didn't know how to locate it or even if the chatter was to be trusted. Eleanor, and I assume, Sam were sent to penetrate the systems, find the problem, and assess the risk."

"I'm guessing that if it got into the wrong hands, it could have been used to take control of a cruise ship and either weaponise it or threaten to do so in a bid to extort money... or worse... to crash it," said Jason.

"Hence the British and American interest," said Sarah.

Rachel nodded. "Eleanor did her research well and then accessed the vulnerability using Bert to get to it. She tested it on the night of the storm before Alex Reyes got to her. Ravanos found blood around a broken piece of metal in the underfloor tunnel. That's what caused the wound Sarah noticed."

"Which is when he must have dropped the micro-SD card," Jason added.

"What's going to happen to poor Bert Holland?" Sarah asked.

Jason frowned, no doubt remembering the possibly innocent nurse.

"He's decided to retire and spend time with his kids. They've lived in Switzerland for ten years now and don't want to return to the UK. He's confirmed that the hospital never traced the nurse who administered the lethal injection." Rachel looked at Jason. "Eleanor used an outside source disguised as a nurse so as not to implicate anyone working in the hospital. It was how she operated."

Jason smiled on hearing that. "Good."

Sarah squeezed Jason's hand before looking at Rachel. "Dare I ask about Sam and Belinda?"

"They have disembarked and will make their own way to their respective homes. Sam needs time to reevaluate his career choice after Eleanor's death. And I doubt our celebrity chef will host any VIP dinners on Queen Cruises in the future."

"That's a shame," said Sarah.

"Greed has its downsides. Her food was delicious, though, and Rosemary enjoyed her galley assignment. The good news is that your husband has shore leave coming up."

"Good for him," Sarah said, looking at Jason, "but I don't."

"Ah, but you do," said Rachel. "When I explained to Graham and Gwen how you could have been killed, they put their heads together and rejigged the duty rota for the next few days. You'll be able to enjoy the next few ports at your leisure."

Sarah's eyes lit up as Jason squeezed her hand. His knuckles were still grazed from his run-in with the security guard.

"What about you, boss? Don't you need some time off?" Jason asked.

"Yes, your chin's very swollen," Sarah said.

"Hopefully it will be well healed by the time Carlos joins me in New York. I'll take a few days' leave then."

"Oh Rachel, that's marvellous news," said Sarah.

Rachel's exhaustion had completely disappeared when Carlos rang to say he had tickets for them to go to Carnegie Hall, and he would join the ship sailing from New York for a week. Plus, she'd be rid of Clint Foster. She smiled at the thought.

"Anyway, you two lovebirds finish your dinner. I've got paperwork to do. One of the joys of being chief of security."

"You're not fooling me," said Jason. "I know you've got a dessert date with Lady Marjorie the Second, Charlotte Kieft."

Rachel rose from the table, laughing. "And that."

"I'm pleased she turned out to be on our side," said Sarah.

"Her help was invaluable," said Rachel, wondering whether there was still more to Charlotte than she realised. "Anyway, I'll catch you later."

THE END

More Rachel Prince adventures coming soon.

AUTHOR'S NOTE

Thank you for reading *Cruise into Darkness* the fourteenth book in the Rachel Prince Mystery series. If you have enjoyed it, please leave an honest review on Amazon and/or any other platform you may use. I love receiving feedback from readers.

Keep in touch:

Signup for my no-spam newsletter and receive a FREE novella. You will also receive news of new releases and special offers and have the opportunity to enter competitions.

https://www.dawnbrookespublishing.com/subscribe

Check out my store for savings and offers:
https://www.dawnbrookesbooks.com

Follow me on Facebook:
https://www.facebook.com/dawnbrookespublishing/
Follow me on YouTube:
https://www.youtube.com/DawnBrookesPublishing

BOOKS BY DAWN BROOKES

Rachel Prince Mysteries

A Cruise to Murder #1

Deadly Cruise #2

Killer Cruise #3

Dying to Cruise #4

A Christmas Cruise Murder #5

Murderous Cruise Habit #6

Honeymoon Cruise Murder #7

A Murder Mystery Cruise #8

Hazardous Cruise #9

Captain's Dinner Cruise Murder #10

Corporate Cruise Murder #11

Treacherous Cruise Flirtation #12

Toxic Cruise Cocktail #13

Cruise into Darkness #14

Lady Marjorie Snellthorpe Mysteries

Death of a Blogger (Prequel Novella)

Murder at the Opera House #1

Murder in the Highlands #2

Murder at the Christmas Market #3

Murder at a Wimbledon Mansion #4

Murder in a Care Home #5

Murder at the Regatta #6

Book 7 Coming soon

Carlos Jacobi PI

Body in the Woods #1

The Bradgate Park Murders #2

The Museum Murders #3

The Clock Tower Murders #4 (Coming soon)

Memoirs

Hurry up Nurse: memoirs of nurse training in the 1970s

Hurry up Nurse 2: London calling

Hurry up Nurse 3: More adventures in the life of a student nurse

ACKNOWLEDGMENTS

Thanks to my beta readers for their comments and suggestions, and for the time they dedicated to reading the early drafts, as well as to my ARC team – I couldn't do without you. A big thank you also goes to my editorial team.

A while ago, I offered readers of my newsletter the opportunity to have their name included as a character in this book. The response was overwhelming, and Charlotte Kieft was randomly selected. Who would have thought you'd become Marjorie the Second? Congratulations and thank you.

I'm also immensely grateful to my immediate circle of family and friends, who remain patient when I'm absorbed in my fictional worlds. Thank you for your continued support in all my endeavours.

I must express my gratitude to my cruise-loving friends for joining me on some of the most precious experiences of my life, and to all the cruise lines for making every holiday a special one.

ABOUT THE AUTHOR

Award-winning author Dawn Brookes holds an MA in Creative Writing with Distinction and is the author of the Rachel Prince Mystery series, combining a unique blend of murder, cruising and medicine with a touch of romance. She has also written the Lady Marjorie Snellthorpe spinoff series and the Carlos Jacobi series, both of which are cozy mysteries.

Dawn has a 39-year nursing pedigree and takes regular cruise holidays, which she claims are for research purposes! She combines these passions with her Christian background and a love of clean crime in her writing.

The surname of Rachel Prince is in honour of her childhood dog, Prince, who used to rest his head on her knee while she lost herself in books.

Dawn's bestselling memoirs outlining her nurse training are available to buy: *Hurry up Nurse: memoirs of nurse training in the 1970s, Hurry up Nurse 2: London calling*, and *Hurry up Nurse 3: More adventures in the life of a student nurse.*

Throughout her career, Dawn worked as a hospital nurse, midwife, district nurse, and a community matron. Before turning to writing for a living, she had multiple articles published in professional journals and co-edited a nursing textbook.

She grew up in Leicester, later moved to London and Berkshire, but now lives in Derby. Dawn holds a Bachelor's degree with Honours and a Master's degree in Education. Writing across genres, she also writes for children. Dawn has a passion for nature and loves animals, especially dogs. Animals will continue to feature in her children's books, as she believes caring for animals and nature helps children become kinder human beings.

Printed in Dunstable, United Kingdom